Harlequin Presents...

Other titles by

# ELIZABETH ASHTON
## IN HARLEQUIN ROMANCES

# ELIZABETH ASHTON

## sanctuary in the desert

*Harlequin Books*

TORONTO • LONDON • NEW YORK • AMSTERDAM • SYDNEY • WINNIPEG

Harlequin Presents edition published March 1977
ISBN 0-373-70679-0

Original hardcover edition published in 1976
by Mills & Boon Limited

Printed in U.S.A.

# CHAPTER ONE

'I THINK it would be marvellous,' Peta Cartwright declared enthusiastically, accepting a cigarette from the pack she was being offered by her neighbour. She did not often smoke, but thought it contributed to the boyish image she cultivated when she was with her fellow students. The youth sitting next to her, Keith Morris, struck a match to light it for her and she accepted the service reluctantly, suspecting a tribute to her sex. Peta was all for women's rights and equality and disdained such small courtesies.

'Of course my parents won't like it,' she went on thoughtfully. 'Poor dears, they still haven't quite eliminated the picture of a homey daughter that they've cherished ever since I was born, but we're as we're made and I can't stick domesticity. I've always been a tomboy.'

'Well, you're over eighteen,' Keith reminded her, 'so they can't do anything to stop you. Your dad ought to sympathise, by all accounts he was full of adventurous spirit in his younger days.'

For Timothy Cartwright had been an explorer and archaeologist, until illness curtailed his activities, and he was well advanced in middle life when he settled down to matrimony and the writing of books about the adventures in which he could no longer participate.

'He always wanted a boy to follow in his footsteps,' Peta said, 'but he left it too late to found a family, I'm the only one who came along, and he ought to realise a daughter's just as good. I'm tough enough to tackle the Arctic or the desert, more so than many boys.'

'I'd say you were!' a second youth, a long-haired,

slightly effeminate-looking creature, said admiringly. 'You can lick me at tennis with one hand tied behind your back.'

'You're a bit of a wilting lily, aren't you, Val?' the fourth member of the party drawled. 'Sure you can stand up to roughing it? This trip won't be a picnic, you know.'

'I mayn't be muscular, but I'm wiry,' Valentine returned good-humouredly, 'and I can hike as far as you can any day, Osric, I've less weight to carry.'

'That's good because we'll hitch-hike and use buses to keep down expenses to a minimum, and we shan't be staying in luxury hotels. We may even be reduced to sleeping out.'

'That's all right by me, Osric, so long as I can bring my guitar.'

'Oh, we'll need that to keep our spirits up,' Keith told him. 'Besides, you might earn a few pennies if you play for our supper.'

'Dirhams,' Peta corrected him, having looked up the currency of the country they proposed to visit, 'and I don't know if the Arabs will appreciate pop music.'

'I bet the young ones do, it's practically universal, but I'll play flamenco, which originated with them—don't forget the south of Spain belonged to Morocco long years ago.'

'What a lot the lad knows,' Keith murmured, 'but what about Peta? Somehow I don't think this expedition will be very suitable for a girl.'

'Oh, rats,' Peta cried scornfully. 'You can just forget I am one. I'm often taken for a boy anyway.'

'Only by the non-observant,' Osric told her slyly, and Peta frowned. She did not like Osric Howarth, who was the only one of her associates who made her aware of her sex. She had caught the speculative gleam in his cold green eyes when he looked at her and it made her squirm. He was the oldest of the quartet and Keith, her special pal, was very much under his thumb. She did not think he was a very

6

good influence over the younger boy and was doing her best to combat it, for she did like Keith, who was a genuine uncomplicated sort of person with a flattering admiration for her sports achievements, for Peta shone not only at tennis and other games but on horseback, swimming and various other sports.

The four of them were students, though not on the same courses, and were discussing their plans for the long summer vacation. Osric had some connection with a shipping firm and had told them he could obtain accommodation for them on a freighter travelling to Morocco if they did not mind a slow journey. From Casablanca they would explore the country, by bus and on foot, staying at youth hostels, there being one in most of the principal towns, which was much the best way to get to know a country.

Peta was eager to go and confident she could stand up to any hardship. She leaned back in her chair—they had met over coffee in their favourite café—and blew smoke rings upwards. Her parents would be definitely anti her plans. Mrs. Cartwright's idea of a foreign holiday was a packaged tour or a stay at a comfortable hotel. That Peta could want to traipse around with three youths in jeans and shirt carrying a knapsack and a sleeping bag would be entirely incomprehensible to her, but she had long since given up doing battle with her hoyden daughter, who abhorred dressing up, deciding she was too old to understand modern youth. She had been approaching forty when Peta was born and thus the generation gap was wider than usual. One of their first clashes had been over her name. Maud Cartwright had romantic ideas and called her child Perdita. At school among the Sarahs, Traceys, Louises and Susans, Perdita had decided that her name was absurd. By deleting the middle three letters she had called herself Peta, and woe betide anyone who was foolish enough to recall her original appellation, for Peta had a fiery temper and a sharp tongue.

7

She grew into a long-legged, flat-chested Amazon of a girl, who excelled at all sports. She was training to be a physical culture teacher, with half an eye on an Olympic championship if she could find enough time to work at it. The pentathlon was her aim.

Keith had been her partner in many of her activities and was useful to ward off amorous approaches from other boys, though he made none himself. Privately they had agreed that love and romance were a useless expenditure of energies that could be diverted into more rewarding channels. Often she suspected he forgot she was not another boy. She never if she could avoid it wore a skirt, always appearing in the unisex garb favoured by most of her colleagues. Mrs. Cartwright had longed for a feminine little girl whom she could dress up in frills and flounces, and often wondered how she had managed to produce this tall coltish creature who was so different from herself and her studious husband. She had never known Timothy Cartwright in his venturesome youth and energetic maturity before his illness sobered him, or she might have realised whence her daughter's wild spirit came.

Peta treated her parents with amused tolerance, considering they were woefully not with modern trends. Her father was absorbed in his writing, her mother had never progressed beyond the Victorian era, the tenets of which she had imbibed from her parents, a country vicar and his parochial wife. Peta had given up trying to make her understand modern pressures and modern ideas and went her own way. She accepted a little unwillingly a moderate allowance from her father 'to see her through college' and augmented it whenever she could with her own earnings, mainly composed of prizes won at sports competitions.

The four of them continued to discuss their plans. Peta had her passport, she had spent, to her mind, a wasted holiday in a French watering place with her mother, except that she had improved her knowledge of the language, which she spoke quite fluently. French was still widely spoken in Morocco, so this accomplishment would be useful. None of them had much money, so expenses would have to be kept to a minimum.

'We'll live rough and eat in native cafés,' Osric proclaimed.

'Drink, you mean,' Valentine corrected him. 'Do they have good wine in Morocco?'

'Only for tourists and export. Moslems are forbidden alcohol. I believe their speciality is mint tea.' Val made a face. 'We'll carry our gear, so we must travel light. Peta won't mind washing out our spare shirts and socks.' Again he threw her a sly glance.

'Peta would mind very much,' she returned, 'we'll do our own chores. I'm not feminine, Osric, so get that idea out of your mind right away, and treat me like another boy.'

'I'll do my best,' he placated her.

Peta turned to Keith her grey eyes sparkling with anticipation. They were her best feature, being large and wide spaced. She wore her dark hair cut shorter than her companions did, and it curled about her well-shaped head and thin face. She had a straight nose and a wide mouth, there was something Egyptian about her brows and jawline, reminiscent of the sculptured heads of Rameses and Nerfertiti.

'At least it's pretty certain to be fine,' she said, 'so we won't need raincoats, but we'd better take a few medicaments.'

'Listen to the explorer's daughter,' Osric murmured satirically, and Peta kicked him.

She did, as she had expected, meet dismayed opposition from her mother; her father merely shrugged his shoulders and observed he supposed she was old enough to know what she was doing.

9

'But alone with three men!' Mrs. Cartwright wailed. 'If there was another girl going it wouldn't be quite so ... so unconventional.'

'Rubbish, who cares about conventions?' Peta exclaimed scornfully. 'And most of the girls I know would be quite useless on this sort of expedition. Keith's going—you know him?'

Mrs. Cartwright had met him and had been put off by his long hair and casual garb which she associated with layabouts. She deplored Peta's taste in young men.

'Are you engaged to him?' she hazarded.

'Sort of,' Peta returned, though they were not, hoping to pacify her.

'I suppose that makes a difference,' Maud Cartwright said doubtfully. Peta agreed it did, though she could not see why.

The voyage out was tedious, for the boat was slow, and uneventful. Even the Bay of Biscay was calm. Peta had her own cabin, there being no other woman aboard, and the three boys shared another. In this connection an episode occurred that was to have far-reaching repercussions. It was a lovely evening, the sun sinking through a scarf of roseate cloud towards the placid sea, the coast of Spain faintly visible on the horizon, as the ship ploughed her way steadily southwards. The two younger boys were entertaining the off-duty crew in their mess with Val's guitar. Peta went down to her cabin to fetch a map of Morocco she wanted to study. As she turned to leave, she found Osric barring her way.

'All this space to yourself,' he commented, looking round the interior, which contained two berths, 'while the three of us are cramped together in quarters no bigger than this. How about letting me move in with you?'

Peta shook her dark head. 'Nothing doing, Osric, but if you're so crowded, couldn't you sleep on deck? You've brought your sleeping bag.'

'I'd be lonely, dear, and I'm sure you must feel lonesome yourself at night. You aren't really committed to Keith, are you? He's still wet behind the ears. Now, you and I——' He advanced into the cabin, his green eyes glittering. 'We could have some real fun together.' He slipped his arm about her waist. 'I could teach you all you need to know.'

She threw off his encircling arm. 'I don't want any of that sort of knowledge, Osric. I'm not that kind of girl.'

'But you *are* a girl, though you try to pretend to be a boy. You must have some female urges. Don't tell me young Keith can satisfy them.'

'I don't like that sort of talk, Osric, so pack it up,' she told him coolly. 'The others accept me as one of themselves and I like to forget I'm female. I came for the adventure and because I prefer boys' company to girls', but I've no time for any mush. Now suppose you get out of my cabin and keep out.'

But Osric could not believe she meant to snub his advances, he had a high opinion of his effect on girls, and most of those he knew were accommodating. So far Peta had ignored his hints and innuendoes, so now he was resolved upon a more direct attack.

'You fancy you're so modern and liberated,' he declared, 'but you're still bound by inhibitions. You're frightened to let yourself go. Why, I dare swear you're still a virgin.'

'Of course I am,' she retorted, 'and so far I've never had any wish to be anything else. I certainly don't want to be initiated by a creature like you! If you're feeling that way, it won't be long before we reach Casablanca where I'm sure you can pick up someone who'll be ready to oblige you.'

Osric pretended to be shocked. 'Really, Peta, what a way to talk! I always understood you'd been well brought up, and that's part of your trouble. I don't want a pick-up, I want you. You're beautiful in a way like a young Amazon

11

or a wild filly, and by God, I'd like to tame you.'

A note of passion crept into his voice and his nostrils flared. Peta was leaning, hands in the pockets of her jeans, against the two-tiered bunks, her grey eyes were almost on a level with his. His simile of an Amazon was very apt, there was something about the way she carried her head, the frank fearlessness of her gaze, that was both challenging and provocative. It would not be difficult to imagine her armed and mounted riding out to do battle for her integrity against the masculine world, a being dedicated to celibacy and the moon goddess.

'I daresay,' she said casually, 'but it would take a better man than you to do that. I'm just not interested.'

'Peta!' He took a step towards her, his eyes alight. 'You don't mean that. I'll show you how much of a man I am.'

She edged away from him. 'Don't you dare to try any caveman stuff with me,' she warned him. 'Among my other accomplishments I've learned judo, and I fancy you'd get the worst of it.'

At last he got the message and retreated to the door glowering.

'I'll get even with you for this, my girl,' he threatened.

'Oh, come, Osric, don't be so theatrical. You'll spoil our trip if you build up a well of resentment. Come on, forget this nonsense and let's be just good friends.'

She held out her hand to him placatingly, but he ignored it.

'Friendship isn't what I want from women,' he said coldly. 'But maybe you'll change your mind later on. I understand hot countries can have an amorous effect upon girls, so perhaps you'll melt.'

'You'd better not count upon that,' she told him. 'I'll be far too interested in the place and its people to have any time for you.'

He went away, and Peta gave a sigh of relief. She hoped

that he would not pester her again, and this was a complication that she had not foreseen. She decided he would find other diversions once they had landed and he was only making a pass at her to relieve the boredom of the voyage. What she did not realise was that Osric's vanity was involved, and that was a very large part of his make-up, and he was on the way to becoming a vindictive enemy. However, he made no further advances and by the time they reached Casablanca she had forgotten the incident.

They were to return on the freighter's next trip a month hence, and confirmed their reservation with the shipping office. They spent their first night on Moroccan soil at a youth hostel in that city. Casablanca, the commercial capital of the country, with its big white modern blocks of buildings, its wide palm-lined streets, was similar to many other towns in the world. It did possess a small medina, a relic of the old town, but they decided to push on next day to a more characteristic environment and took the bus to Rabat. The road crossed flat dun-coloured country intersected by dried-up wadis under a white-hot sky. It was bordered by eucalyptus trees. There Peta saw her first camels, a string of small mangy-looking animals that were far from impressive. Rabat, the political capital, was much more so. Here too there was an old and a new town, the latter having been built by the French. The walled Medina stood above the banks of a river, and the enormous Hassan Tower built on a small hill above the river marshes dominated the scene. Beyond the town was the beach and the wide spaces of the Atlantic Ocean, where they went down to bathe.

Being the only one of the party who was fluent in French, Peta took the lead in asking for accommodation, information and shopping. French was Morocco's second language and nearly everyone they encountered knew at least a few words. In the souks she bought herself an Arab d'jel-

13

laba, a voluminous gown with a hood. It was expensive and Keith rebuked her for extravagance, but she pointed out that it would have many uses, not least to protect her from the dust, which seemed to be everywhere when the wind blew, and its pointed hood would shelter her from the sun, since she hated sunglasses. It was also a complete disguise. Rabat was full of tourists of all nationalities, and in addition to its Arab population there was still a large French colony. Though the older women still wore the haik, a white tent-like garment, and occasionally a veil, the young ones were adopting European clothes, and especially the younger men, the universal jeans and shirt replacing their former picturesque robes.

They were bound for Tangier and decided to walk part of the way up the coast, taking the bus when they became tired, bathing when so inclined and sleeping in native lodgings. Nobody took much notice of them, for the inhabitants were used to seeing groups of hippies roaming the countryside and rarely noted them individually. Osric let his beard grow, Valentine tried to do likewise, but he had little hair on his cherubic countenance. Keith shaved when he could to keep Peta company, for most of the people they spoke to thought she was another boy. She grew lean and hard, and in spite of the discomfort of dust and insects was always in high spirits.

Tangier delighted her with its Grand Socco, the market filled with stalls selling fruit, flowers and other things supervised by Berber women from the Rif in brightly coloured clothes with huge round hats and striped aprons. From the Socco a jumble of streets and houses flowed down to the sea, while above it the ancient kasbah looked out above the walls of the Medina over the straits to Spain. They bathed off sandy beaches where the grey waters of the Atlantic met the blue of the Mediterranean Sea.

Peta was insistent that they must see something of the

14

Rif mountains, and they obtained a lift in a truck as far as Tetouan, the former capital of the Spanish zone. They travelled through green open country until going over a pass they approached the Rif proper and Tetouan could be seen hanging like a cloud on the mountainside. From Tetouan they went by bus to Chaouen or Chechaouen, through a country of vast open spaces and softly rounded mountains. Chaouen was once a sacred city and barred to strangers, but it had now become a tourist centre. It was at the top of a side road that wound steeply upwards and above it rose a mountain. Like all Moroccan towns it had twentieth-century additions, but these had charm which many others did not. White walls and pantiled roofs enclosed half revealed gardens filled with flowers including many British favourites, roses, dahlias, antirrhinums, delphiniums, montbretia and pansies, while nasturtiums and honeysuckle sprawled everywhere. Double rows of trees gave shade to the streets, the inner row being orange trees laden with the bitter fruit that nobody seemed to want.

Above the houses and the trees were the flanks of a great mountain, its sharp crest cutting the blue sky, but it was the old town that distinguished Chaouen. As in all medinas the streets were very narrow and went through tunnels where houses had been built on arches that buttressed the close-spaced walls. In its centre was an open square by the castle that had fallen into ruin, and now enclosed nothing more sinister than a garden. Women in white haiks brought their children to play there in the cooler part of the day, and there were children everywhere, bright-eyed, brown-skinned little imps wearing fezes or woollen caps.

The Tourist Board had put the once forbidden city on the map and enlarged the Parador hotel for visitors. Its tarif was beyond Peta and her friends, who found lodgings with an Arab family who let rooms. They did treat themselves to a drink on the Parador Terrace, from which they had a superb view of soaring mountains, terraced wheat fields, orchards and olive groves, but the familiar palm trees of the lowlands were absent from the riot of fig, almond, orange, pomegranate and mulberry trees.

On their second morning, the three youths decided they wanted to climb the mountain behind the town. Peta did not think they would get far and for once declined to accompany them, saying it was much too hot to scramble over rocks and she felt like having an easy day. She washed her hair, and did some repairs to their garments; she had intended to launder their spare shirts and socks in spite of her declaration that they were each to do their own chores. The boys, especially Keith, were not very adept at such tasks, so she decided to take pity on them, but their hostess as soon as she grasped her intention would not hear of her doing so, and went off with the garments to do them herself.

After a frugal lunch of unleavened bread, cheese and a lemon drink Peta set off for a walk away from the town down a winding path that seemed to lead into a valley. The hood of her d'jellaba protected her head and neck and she belted it about her waist in a very un-native manner to prevent it flapping in the breeze. She had traversed about a mile when the sound of hooves behind her caused her to draw off the narrow path behind a clump of bushes to leave room for the animals' passage. Two riders went by mounted on splendid horses. One was a woman, her face concealed by dark glasses under her hat, but she was young and well formed, as her elegant jodhpurs showed. The other was a man, spare and brown, his arms and neck, which were bare, burned to the colour of tan teak. A white sombrero shaded his face and nape. As they passed her, Peta caught the words, *'vacances'* and *'merveilleux'*. They were evidently a French couple holidaymaking and having a wonderful time. Some way further ahead she came upon the two horses tethered to a tree, but there was no sign of their riders. Peta smiled a little contemptuously; for them marvellous holidays were not complete without a spot of lovemaking, a need she had not experienced. She had gone about another half mile when the sound of hooves again fell on her ears. Looking behind her, she saw that one of the horses had broken loose and was coming towards her at a fast trot, its reins dangling dangerously before it. She knew the hazard and felt it would be a shame if such a fine animal were to put its foot in them and come down. Instinctively she started forward and caught the loose reins as the beast shied violently, throwing up its head.

'Whoa, my beauty!'

For a moment it seemed it would jerk the reins out of her hands or drag her to the ground as it pulled against them, but she continued to speak soothingly and eventually the animal stood still. Peta caressed the glossy neck while she regarded it admiringly. It was a powerful animal, sixteen hands tall, blood and fire in every inch of it with the small head and full eyes of the Arab strain. Peta was assailed by temptation. She had not been on a horse for several months and she was passionately fond of riding. Hitching up her gown, she put her foot in the stirrup and swung herself into the saddle. The stirrups were too long for her and she pushed her feet through the leathers. The animal started forward down the path at a fast pace and she had difficulty in controlling it. She would have liked to give it its head, but the path was too steep and narrow to be safe to gallop. When she had obtained complete control of it, she reluctantly turned about to retrace their steps, for its owner would be looking for it.

A piercing whistle caused the horse to prick up its ears and break into a canter. Rounding a corner, Peta came upon the French couple, the man leading the other horse upon which the lady was mounted. Peta managed to bring her steed to halt a few paces in front of them and as she slid to the ground the woman cried:

'*Voilà, le petit voleur!*'

'Hush, Yvette,' the man said, also in French, 'I do not think the *garçon* meant to steal Mustapha—you see he has brought him back.'

Somewhat haltingly Peta explained that she had intercepted the beast; something about this couple made her feel shy and her voice was low and husky. Yvette was looking accusingly at the streaks of foam on Mustapha's neck.

'Téo, he has overridden him,' she said indignantly.

'That was probably Mustapha's fault,' Téo excused her. 'He can pull like the devil, but I am surprised he allowed a stranger to mount him.'

'I . . . I'm used to horses,' Peta mumbled, feeling guilty.

'You must be.' He took off his hat, revealing close-cut brown hair almost the same colour as his skin, and fanned himself with it, for the sun was still hot. Glancing at him surreptitiously, Peta saw that he was not a very big man, although several inches taller than herself, having the true horseman's lean slight figure. Big men are often slightly lethargic as if all their strength has gone in growth, but this man was electric with nervous vitality; there did not appear to be an inch of fat on his spare muscular body. His eyes flickered over her indifferently and she saw they were also brown flecked with gold so that they appeared tawny, keen hawk's eyes under slightly prominent brows.

'My husband will not be pleased to learn that his best stallion has been mishandled by *un paysan*,' the woman complained, thereby revealing that her escort was not her spouse.

'He would be still more displeased if Mustapha had fallen and broken his knees,' Téo told her, while he ran his hands over the horse's legs. 'If anyone is to blame it is I for my carelessness in not making him more secure. Luckily he

18

is not even scratched, and we owe this *jeune garçon* our thanks. You are a tourist, *monsieur*?' He eyed her mixed garb with a puzzled expression. Her speech betrayed that she was not a native, and although he had seen plenty of drop-outs and hippies wandering about the country, she did not look as though she belonged to that genre. Her hood had fallen back during her ride, and her black curly head emerged from the folds about her neck. As she answered his question with a vague 'Sort of,' he met her clear grey eyes and his face contracted in a spasm, while his colour ebbed.

'*Nom de dieu!*' he muttered, and drew his hand across his brow.

'*Qu'est-ce que c'est*, Téo?' Yvette asked anxiously. 'Are you ill?'

'*Ce n'est rien*,' he returned smiling wryly. 'Merely a spectre from the past. *Enfin, mon garçon*,' he put his hand in his pocket and pulled out a handful of money from which he selected two ten dirham notes. 'Let me discharge my obligation.' He held them out to Peta.

Her first impulse was to refuse, but recalling that they were travelling on a shoe string, she took them with a murmur of thanks. Téo gathered up the reins and swung himself into the saddle with a quick lithe movement. Peta stepped back out of range of the dancing hooves as Mustapha expressed his impatience to be off. Yvette threw her a scornful glance and urged her mount to a trot, disappearing up the path without a backward look, but Téo turned his head and raised his hand in salutation before he followed her.

Peta watched them out of sight with an odd feeling of regret. The Frenchman was a man after her own heart and he made her three companions, even Osric, seem immature. She was not surprised that he had taken her for a boy; most people did at first sight and she had deliberately fostered that impression. Téo would not expect to find a girl wan-

19

dering about alone or to have been able to manage his spirited horse—moreover, she had not raised her voice during their short exchange. Normally she would be gratified by his mistake, but she caught herself wishing that he had known her real sex, though that could have made no difference, except that possibly his reaction might have been more positive betraying greater interest.

As she was a female, she was curious about his relationship with the, from her point of view, unpleasant young woman he was accompanying. From what she had overheard he was spending a holiday in the vicinity, and appeared to be escorting his hostess in her husband's absence. No harm in that, except that they had tethered their horses while they wandered off ... to admire the view? Was that likely? She thought not, and then shook herself mentally; it was none of her business what they were doing and she was unlikely to see them again, but she felt faintly regretful that the fascinating Téo had not found a companion more worthy of him, for from what she had been able to see of Yvette she had not appeared attractive and her voice was high and shrill.

Peta returned to the old town and sat moodily watching the children playing in the kasbah garden, wishing she had gone with the boys. She felt both restless and lonely and even her beautiful surroundings did not solace her. For the first time their gypsy mode of travel discontented her. She would like to have been staying at the Parador, the comparative luxury of which she had glimpsed from the terrace, or at some private house with all the amenities and gorgeous horses to ride, and realised her unrest had been evoked by Téo. Bother the man! Upon closer acquaintance he would probably prove to be disillusioning, and it was unlike her normal unimpressionable self to allow a man's handsome face to so disturb her. Like some silly little teenager with a crush on a pop singer, she told herself witheringly. Nor was Téo strikingly handsome, only arresting, and being a sophisticated Frenchman he would have no use for a shabbily dressed English girl who tried to ape a youth. She recalled that Yvette had worn beautifully tailored jodhpurs and a silk shirt and the contrast between their appearances must have been pitiful.

As the colours of the sunset began to flame in the sky, Peta returned to their lodgings and gave herself a cold sponge bath. Arrayed only in her underclothes and the ubiquitous d'jellaba, she was sitting in the courtyard around which the rooms of the house were built when the mountaineers returned. She knew now why Easterners favoured long loose garments; they were much the coolest wear. The trio were hot, tired and disgruntled; they had not progressed far up the mountain.

'You were the sensible one,' Keith told her. 'What have you been doing? Just lazing?'

'More or less.' She found she was reluctant to mention her meeting with Téo and his girl-friend. The incident seemed personal to herself alone.

Osric laid an ugly-looking plant across her knees and she examined it without much interest. It had dull green leaves and a spike like brown feathers.

'What is it?' she asked.

'Cannabis satavia, otherwise Indian hemp. It's used for making ropes . . . and hashish.'

'Oh!' She dropped the plant distastefully. 'It grows here?'

'In profusion. Its cultivation is supposed to be controlled, but a lot of the places in the Rif are inaccessible. Smuggling is a flourishing trade here.'

'They get a stiff sentence if they're caught,' Keith remarked. 'I'd hate to sample a Moroccan prison.'

'Only fools get caught,' Osric said contemptuously, 'and it's an easy way to make a lot of money, especially smuggling diamonds.'

'Oh, come off it—diamonds! You're romancing,' Peta laughed.

'I'm not. They bring them up from the south through the desert, stolen in the first place, naturally. It's not difficult. The hardest part is getting them through Customs at the port of disembarkation.'

Peta looked at him uneasily. 'I hope you're not thinking of doing anything so stupid.'

'Me? Who'd entrust me with diamonds?' He laughed, but the laugh was forced.

Their hostess brought them their supper, bowls of soup, a native concoction that appeared with variations on most native menus. It was composed of diced mutton, chicken offal, chick peas, ginger, onion, saffron and spices, which was cooked for at least two hours and then had added to it seasoned rice and finally tomatoes, butter and bread yeast. The smiling Berber woman was pleased by their praise of her cooking.

After the meal they wandered out into the scented dusk to watch the last of the day gilding the mountain crests. Osric soon left them, saying he was seeing someone in the Medina.

'One of his smuggling pals,' Keith said flippantly.

Val looked at him reproachfully.

'He'd never try that on. He's very keen on getting to know the people.'

'I've seen him talking to some weird-looking types,' Keith informed them. 'Murderous-looking characters. I hope he doesn't end by getting his throat cut.'

'Not him!' Peta exclaimed. 'If anyone can look after himself, it's Osric, and he wouldn't scruple to sell out a pal to save his own skin.'

Val, who hero-worshipped Osric, began to defend him hotly and Peta hastened to placate him, saying she had not meant what she said. She little knew that her words had been prophetic.

From the Rif they wandered down to Fez, where they found accommodation at another youth hostel, and there they stayed. There was a great deal to see, for Fez is a beautiful city surrounded on every side by hills, possessing both an old and a new section, both ringed by a continuous line of mud ramparts, and contained some magnificent examples of Moorish architecture. It had a vast medina, an enormous labyrinth where the unwary could easily become lost. Its modern town was not much better. Keith and Peta saw little of the other two. Taking Val with him, Osric spent the greater part of their nights in the medina. He said they were earning a few dirhams by singing in cafés. Peta would have liked to move on to South Morocco, but Osric and Val refused to leave, and Keith thought they had better not split up. So they contented themselves with an excursion to Meknes and the Roman ruins at Volubilis. But Keith too seemed to have found some personal interest, for he often left her on some mysterious errand, and Peta was forced to wander about on her own. She did not mind; when she was disguised in the enveloping folds of her d'jellaba few people realised she was a girl.

Then when the time for their departure drew near, Keith exploded a bombshell. He wanted to stay in Morocco and study Arabic. The British Council had promised to find him a job teaching English at one of the universities of which there were several in Fez, and he had cancelled his passage on the boat home.

'You'll be all right, won't you?' he asked Peta with some belated twinges of conscience. 'You're not one of those silly girls who need a man to conduct them everywhere and you'll have Osric and Val with you on the journey home. Fact is I've fallen in love with this country and I don't want to leave it.'

23

Since their code was that everybody should live their own life in their own way, Peta offered no protest, but she felt distressed. Though she was not in love with him Keith had always been such a good friend.

'You must do what you want to do, of course,' she told him. 'But I'll miss you terribly.'

'It won't be for ever. I'll be coming home some time,' he pointed out. 'And I'll write when I can find time.'

Peta doubted if he would; their coterie were not strong on correspondence and relied upon the telephone for communication. She said goodbye to him feeling sure that their relationship had ended.

On their return journey their ship was making a detour to include a call at Gibraltar and Peta was looking forward to seeing the Rock. She was put out when Osric and Val told her upon the eve of their departure that they had arranged to disembark there, leaving her to continue the voyage alone.

'You don't mind, do you, Peta?' Osric asked, adding nastily, 'It isn't as if you enjoyed my company.'

'Oh, I can manage,' she assured him, aware of a vague disquiet. 'But haven't you booked your passages home?'

'The shipping company will make a refund when we get back to London. Val and I want to hitch-hike through Spain, and I've some contacts I want to make, friends of friends I made in Fez. I don't suppose you'd want to come with us, and you have to get back to start your new term, don't you?'

So for that matter should he, but that was not her business. She noticed that he would not meet her eyes and had an oddly furtive expression.

'Yes, I do, and I certainly wouldn't want to wander about Spain with you,' she said a little tartly, for she resented their desertion.

Then he did look at her with a malicious glint in his

24

green eyes.

'Perhaps you'll come to regret having snubbed me,' he told her darkly. 'When I'm a rich man.'

'I didn't know you had expectations.'

'You don't know a lot of things, my lovely Amazon. All you dream of is gold medals. Well, it will be goodbye at Gibraltar, for I don't expect we'll meet again.'

Peta's uneasiness grew as he left her. Osric was hatching something, but it was nothing to do with her and she would be glad when she had seen the last of him.

# CHAPTER TWO

THE road between Casablanca and Marrakech is some hundred and fifty miles of fast travel straight across an arid plain. Peta was traversing it in the back of a covered truck concealed among bulky sacks in baking discomfort. She had wanted to visit South Morocco, but she had never imagined it would be in such extraordinary circumstances.

The events at the docks were a medley of confused impressions in her mind in which three faces stood out with painful clarity: Osric's, when he realised that contrary to the usual procedure a strict check was being made of everybody's baggage. He had turned a sickly green as he muttered to her:

'The strap of your knapsack is undone.'

It was slung on her back over her d'jellaba which she was wearing as the easiest way to carry it.

'Leave it,' she had said as he fumbled with it, 'I'll soon have to open it.'

He had pushed past her ungallantly, shepherding Val, and that was the last she saw of them.

The next was that of the Customs official as he discovered the incriminating little package full of white stones. He had given a grunt of satisfaction accompanied by a nasty look.

Finally that of the man called Téo. How he came to be at the docks in Casablanca when she had last seen him in the Rif was beyond her understanding, but he was there, and the Archangel Gabriel could not have been more welcome in her distress.

Peta protested incoherently that she knew nothing about

the packet, that it must have been planted upon her, but her words had fallen upon unresponsive ears. A stalwart gendarme placed himself at her side, and sheer horror at her predicament engulfed her.

Then there had been a sudden disturbance, a crowd of panic-stricken people surged back from the quays ... shouts ... screams ... a bomb? A highjack? She did not know, but in the split second during which her captor's attention was diverted from her she wriggled like an eel past her guard and plunged into the crowd.

Then she had sighted Téo standing like a rock amid the surge of humanity impassively watching its turmoil, unperturbed and unafraid. Some instinct urged her to struggle towards him and clutch his arm.

'Help me, *monsieur*!' she had pleaded, strangely confident that he would, her big grey eyes full of desperate appeal gazing up at him beseechingly.

The same curious spasm that she had noticed before at Chaouen contorted his face.

'The boy who saved my horse!' he exclaimed in French, recognising her at once. '*Que faites vous?*'

'*Monsieur*, I'm in trouble.'

His face hardened. '*Vous passez contrebande?*'

'*Non—oui—monsieur, aidez-moi!*' she implored.

The shrill blast of a police whistle set her trembling.

'Little fool!' he ejaculated. '*Eh bien*,' his hand closed over her wrist, 'come with me. No, don't run, walk quickly.'

He guided her through a maze of passages and dim warehouses, until they came out into a loading bay beside which a covered truck was drawn up. He looked from left to right, but there was no one in sight. Porters, loaders and guards had rushed off to the scene of the scare.

'*Dans la derrière*,' the Frenchman whispered, and heaved her up over the high tailboard of the truck. Inside was a miscellaneous collection of articles, cartons, packages, some

27

machinery and several large sacks.

'Lie still behind the baggage,' he went on in a penetrating under tone, 'until we are out of the town. I've
obtained my Customs clearance and am ready to leave, but
my man seems to have joined the bomb-seekers, but don't
worry, I'm well known here and nobody will try to stop
me.'

Peta crouched down behind the sacks, intent only upon
escaping from the docks. All the macabre tales the boys had
delighted to tell of the horrors of Moroccan prisons and the
long sentences dealt to smugglers recurring to her.

The Frenchman whom his lady friend had called Téo
shouted for Hassan and running footsteps answered him.
The man addressed his master excitedly in a gabble of
mixed languages describing the incident that had facilitated
her escape, but she could not make out what particular
hazard of modern travel had caused the rumpus, from
Téo's contemptuous comments it seemed it had only been a
false alarm, but she was more than grateful to whoever had
started it. Finally Téo became impatient and curtly bade
his henchmen get a move on or words to that effect, and the
two men climbed into the cab. The engine started and the
truck lumbered away through the dock gates without being
challenged.

As the truck rumbled through the streets of Casablanca,
Peta's panic subsided and she began to think connectedly.

It was obvious what had happened. Osric had been carrying contraband and had planted the packet in her haversack
when he fumbled with the strap. He had not expected to be
stopped and his one idea had been to get rid of it. She
recalled the waxen pallor of his face when he had spoken to
her; he had been in a deadly funk.

If she had waited and managed to get her story across, he
might have been arrested before he embarked, but of course
he would deny complicity and it would have been her word

28

against his, so she would not have gained anything. Her appearance, she knew, would have been against her. So many scruffy youngsters tried to smuggle stuff out of Morocco, though usually they were caught when landing in Spain. Someone must have given the *douane* a tip-off and that was why there had been this close check.

Osric would tell the captain of their ship that she too had changed her plans as Keith had done and Val was too much under his thumb to protest, so there was no help to be had from that quarter. Osric intended to abandon her to her fate without scruple.

Poor, foolish youth, he had succumbed to the poison of the East, and what moral sense he had had been destroyed. Peta dismissed the unsavoury subject to consider the Frenchman Téo, who had impulsively saved her, and whether his action had been wise. It might have been more sensible to appeal to the British Consul, but the evidence was very much against her and it might have been several days before he could be contacted, and meanwhile she would have been in custody. She shuddered at the thought of the indignities she might have had to suffer. Why, she wondered vaguely, had Téo so providentially been at the docks in Casablanca when she had last seen him many miles away? Her situation had all the incongruity of a nightmare, and she would wake up in the safety of her bed in the hostel at Casablanca.

Unfortunately it was no dream but a grim reality as the day grew hotter towards noon and her position became more uncomfortable. All she could see by raising her head was a strip of white-hot sky over the tailboard. She dared not move in case she made herself visible to whatever was following them, if anything was.

She heard the swish of other vehicles as they went past. Occasionally the driver of another truck shouted out a greeting to which Hassan replied. She heard the name of

29

Allah invoked more than once requesting His protection. She prayed for it also, although she did not call Him Allah.

Where was she being taken and what would become of her? She had nothing besides the clothes she wore, a comb and some loose change in her pocket; everything else had been confiscated, and they seemed to be driving into the heart of Africa. Overcome with heat and misery, she had fallen into a kind of stupor when she became aware that the truck had stopped and a form, dark against the brightness of the sky outside, was climbing over the tailboard. Her hand flew to her mouth to stifle a scream, then she recognised it as Téo. From outside came the murmur of voices. It was the hour of midday prayer.

'*Eh bien*, so you're still alive?' he inquired. 'I've brought you something to drink. It's only Coca-Cola, I'm afraid, it's the best I could obtain for you. Also a few dates.'

He prised the top off the bottle and handed it to her. She drank greedily, for the dry heat had made her terribly thirsty.

'Thank you, that saved my life,' she said huskily. Unthinkingly she had spoken in English and he replied in the same tongue with only a slight accent.

'So you are British? I might have guessed. I suppose you're one of those young drop-outs who make a nuisance of themselves wandering around without adequate means. Surprising you knew how to handle a horse. What were you carrying?'

'I don't know. It looked like a collection of white stones.'

'Diamonds!' he exclaimed. 'No wonder the Customs were on the alert.' Peta recalled what Osric had said about the stones being brought up through the desert from the mines and guessed he had met his contact in Fez. 'But what do you mean by saying you didn't know?' Téo demanded.

'Honestly I didn't. They were planted on me.'

'You mean someone asked you to take a parcel out and

30

you'd no more sense than to fall for that trick?' he asked.

'No, it was put in my luggage without my knowledge.'

He looked at her dubiously and she doubted that he believed her. Then he shrugged his shoulders and asked:

'What will you do now? I'm on my way to Marrakech. From there we could contact the British Consulate, or have you friends you could go to?'

She had no friend except Keith in Fez, and he could not help her. She said nervously: 'I've no friends here, and the Consul won't be sympathetic as I've no money nor passport and he'd probably insist upon turning me over to the authorities. Do you live in Marrakech?'

'No, my place is over the Atlas in a desert oasis called Dar el Bali, which means old castle. I'm an engineer and a mineralologist, employed on irrigation and prospecting. When I met you at Chaouen I was enjoying a much needed leave with my good friends the Daumiers. It's infernally hot in the desert at this time of year.'

'No one would look for me at this Dar ... what you said,' she told him eagerly, 'and I could be quite useful if you keep horses.'

He was silent, seemingly taken aback by her suggestion, nor was she certain what had prompted her to make it. She had much of her father in her and his mention of the desert had excited her; she had never expected to have a chance to see it. She knew nothing about this man, but there seemed to be a sort of affinity between them and instinctively she trusted him. Moreover, fate seemed determined to throw them together, since she had encountered him both at Chaouen and Casablanca. In that country the people were great believers in fate.

At length he spoke. 'I don't keep horses, and it's a cruel sun-blasted land I'm going to. No marble palaces or luxurious tents as you may have read about in romances, only mud castles, sand dunes, red rocks and dusty palms. But

31

you're welcome to sample it if you wish. As you say, no one will look for you there and I can probably make use of you.'

'I'd be glad to do anything I could.'

Far from antagonising her, his description had increased her interest. She recalled that her father had said the land beyond the Anti Atlas was a unique country.

'You'll have to work,' he said succinctly. 'I've no use for idlers. For the present, Hassan is having a siesta, we are resting here for the hottest part of the day. He doesn't know we have a passenger, so you must stay hidden until we reach Marrakech, but I'll make you a little more comfortable.'

He moved the sacks so that she could sit upon one and receive what air came in over the tailboard without being visible from outside.

'These are our month's stores, mine and the Caid's,' he explained. 'But it was the pump I went to fetch from the docks; it had been exported to me to Casa, fortunately for you.'

'Very fortunately,' Peta agreed thankfully.

He went on to tell her that he had a friend who lived outside Marrekech who would put them up for the night. She was the widow of a cousin of his and could be trusted. Tomorrow he would tell Hassan he had picked up another cousin who wanted to visit Dar el Bali. 'Then you won't have to travel any further among the meal sacks,' he concluded.

'Why are you doing so much for me?' she asked impulsively. 'You despise me, and yet you saved me.'

'Hush, keep your voice low,' he warned her. Then he grinned, a flash of white teeth in his brown face, shaded by the hood of the truck.

'*Alors*, I owe you a good turn for recovering Mustapha. I should hate to have caused harm to one of Gustave Daum-

32

ier's horses. He's a good friend of mine—besides, no one whom Mustapha tolerated could be irredeemable.' Peta smiled faintly, at this original way of assessing character. 'Also,' he went on, relapsing into French, '*vos yeux*, they remind me of ... someone ...' his words trailed away and he stared bleakly out of the back of the truck, presenting towards Peta his aquiline profile, with its slightly hooked nose, firmly moulded chin and mobile mouth, the brows protruding slightly over the dark-lashed tawny eyes, giving him a hawklike appearance.

'*Mon dieu*,' he muttered, 'but I am a sentimental fool!' The eagle glance returned to her. 'And you, *mon garçon*, will no doubt turn out to be a great embarrassment to me.'

*Mon garçon*—he still believed she was a boy, and if a lad would be an embarrassment how much more so would be a girl, but she did not dare to undeceive him, not yet. His misapprehension afforded her some sort of protection.

'*Alors*,' he went on briskly, 'tell me your name. Mine is Théodore (he pronounced it Téodor) d'Argentière. As I said, I work for the Moroccan Government. What are you called?'

'Peta.'

'Peter what?'

She hesitated. Her father's books were read all over the world, Théodore d'Argentière might possibly have heard of him, and her escapade would reflect no credit upon the family name. Her parents had opposed this expedition to Morocco and her natural independence shrank from involving them in her stupid folly.

'Brown,' she said. 'I'm a student.'

'A pity you don't confine your activities to your studies,' he told her drily. '*Enfin*, we'd better translate your name into French since you are to be my cousin. I will give you asylum, Pierre Brun, until the police have stopped looking for you and the Caid, that is to say the man in charge of

Dar el Bali is my good friend, he will ask no questions. *Maintenant* you must endure until we reach Marrakech and Madame Sancé's house. Your quarters are no worse than the prison cell that threatens you, but you will soon be released.'

'*Monsieur*, I don't know how to thank you,' Peta exclaimed. An impulse towards honesty caused her to add, 'But I think I should tell you ...'

Hassan shouted from outside, cutting short the confession she was about to make.

'*Excusez-moi*,' Téo apologised. 'I am needed.'

He vaulted lightly over the tailboard, leaving Peta with the inadequate refreshment, her new seat near the tailboard, and her unuttered admission, which upon reflection she decided was better not made.

Marrakech was reached as the shadows grew long, its approach heralded by groves of palm trees. The Berber city was the hub of the plain of Haouz which radiated from its red walls. Its most prominent feature, the Koutoubia Tower, was a landmark for miles, rising against the backdrop of the mountains. Peta could see little of it through her restricted viewpoint between the high board and the roof of the truck. Téo circled the old city, heading for the Ouarzazate road, which town was their next stop. Peta glimpsed from time to time the high walls pierced by their tall gateways glowing in the rays of the setting sun. Someway beyond them the truck turned off the highway into a quiet cul-de-sac and came to a halt before a modern white stone villa. It was growing dark and Peta leaned her head wearily against the side of the truck, thankful for the cessation of its motion. She was very tired and hungry, having eaten nothing except the dates since her breakfast in Casa which seemed a hundred years ago. Téo must be explaining her presence to his friend. Eventually he came to the back of the truck, flashing a torch over her.

'You can come out now,' he told her, lowering the tail-board. Peta clambered out with alacrity. In spite of her fatigue her eyes were caught by the glittering line of the mountains, the crests of which were illuminated by the last of the light.

'The Haut Atlas?' she queried.

'Yes, the highest mountains in Morocco, and believe me or not, there are ski resorts among them where one can ski as late as June.'

Peta stared at the summits of bare rock, palely gleaming against the deepening purple of the night sky. This was an aspect of the country that had not occurred to her. Sweating in the dry heat, the thought of snow-covered pistes was as tantalising as a desert mirage to a thirst-crazed man; but Téo broke rudely into her contemplation, seizing her firmly by the arm and hustling her round the corner of the house towards the rear of it through a shrubbery of tamarisk and oleander.

'Madame Sancé has put a room at your disposal,' he told her curtly. 'Kindly don't leave it without permission. Food will be brought to you and we shall continue our journey early in the morning.'

'Your orders shall be obeyed, my lord.'

He glanced at her sharply through the gathering shadows, suspecting sarcasm.

'I won't stand any cheek from you, *mon gosse*.'

'None was intended,' she retorted, again deciding to maintain her deception. He might try to dump her upon this unknown woman if he discovered her sex, and she was determined to go on to the desert country. 'I was only expressing my complete submission to your orders,' she concluded.

'Keep it up, then, and we shan't quarrel,' he bade her.

They reached a side door and he pushed her through it and that of a small room just inside, switching on the light.

The room was comfortably furnished with a divan bed and a fitted basin with running water and commode. A slatted blind was drawn over the window.

'How very civilised,' Peta remarked pleasantly surprised.

'Most amenities are to be had here,' he informed her. 'The tourist trade is valuable. You will find life very much more primitive at Dar el Bali. Ah, Zillah!' He turned swiftly as a woman appeared carrying a tray. 'It is good of you to bring food for my waif and stray yourself.' He addressed her in French.

'I thought the fewer who knew about your *protégé* the better,' Zillah explained in the same language.

Peta beheld a plump, dark-haired woman wearing a kaftan over Moorish trousers. Although she might be French she evidently felt Eastern dress became her and she looked as if she might be of mixed blood. On her feet were the heelless babouches, the slippers favoured by the country, and jewels sparkled in her ears and at her throat. She had a flimsy tinsel-trimmed veil over her head and her eyes were black and lustrous. Her whole appearance was very much the European idea of an Eastern odalisque, and Téo appeared to appreciate it, for his tawny eyes gleamed. Peta instinctively wrapped the folds of her gown about her more closely, aware that it would be more difficult to deceive a woman's eye than an uninterested male. Her hood had fallen back to display her dark curly head, and her face was pale with fatigue and smeared with dirt.

'Surely he is very young to be such a reprobate,' Zillah Sancé observed, smiling. 'A beardless boy.'

'They start young nowadays,' Téo returned with eyes only for Zillah's opulence, 'but I hope he's not too old to be reformed.'

Zillah giggled. 'I'm sorry for you, *mon petit*, if Téo intends to discipline you.' She threw the man a coquettish look. 'You can be a bit of a brute, *mon ami*.'

'It's sometimes necessary to be harsh, but I trust I'm always just,' Téo told her. 'Come, *chérie*, the lad needs food and sleep, and I have a lot to say to you. *Bonsoir, garçon*.'

He nodded carelessly to Peta and with his arm about Zillah's substantial waist led her out of the room.

The food was an ample helping of mutton and rice, and a dish of fruit. There was also a large jug of lemonade; Zillah was generous with her hospitality. She seemed to be finding consolation for her widowhood; *chérie* meant darling. Peta remembered the other woman at Chaouen, who, though she had a husband, had shown a markedly possessive manner towards Téo. He made good use of his feminine admirers, holidays in the Rif, luxurious accommodation at Marrakech, and possibly he received other benefits.

Peta washed her hands and face, promising herself more extensive ablutions when she had eaten. She devoured the food with appetite, for she was very hungry. The meal despatched except for some of the fruit—there were figs, oranges, peaches and grapes—she stripped and luxuriated in an all-over wash. She rinsed out her underwear, knowing it would be dry by morning, the aertex garments betraying no femininity. A loose white gown had been provided for her which she put on gratefully, rejoicing in its cleanliness and the faint smell of attar of roses that emanated from it. She also washed her hair, and while she rubbed it dry, Téo d'Argentière and his lady friends again invaded her thoughts. He had struck her as a man of integrity, but being human, he could not be blamed for accepting relaxation where it offered itself when he came in from his wilderness, and Zillah, she judged, would have no scruples. As for Yvette Daumier, that relationship was probably quite innocent. At least she herself would present no temptation when, as must happen eventually, her sex was revealed.

She sighed and stared at what she could see of herself in

the mirror. 'Heavens, what a gawk!' she exclaimed aloud, not noticing the shapeliness of her long graceful limbs attractively tanned by the hot sun, nor the fine contours of her head and shoulders. Téo obviously liked plump feminine curves and would find no allure in a tall lanky creature who looked so like the boy she aped. She did not normally grieve over her lack of figure, but tonight she found herself wishing she had some of Zillah's obvious sexiness. Then Téo might notice her ... she checked her thoughts sternly. Their present situation would be untenable if he did and he would never have brought her out of Casa if he had known she was a girl.

Peta slept at once exhausted by her experiences. Towards morning the dry heat made her restless and she began to dream, phantoms of Osric, Keith and Téo intermingling with scenes of assault and violence. She awoke in a sweat of terror to a pale dawn and for a while lay still trying to recall where she was and what had happened. Osric's spiteful face still seemed to float before her vision. Then she remembered he was far away and his plans had miscarried. She was safe, due to the intervention of a quixotic Frenchman, and though her future was hazardous in the extreme she was oddly confident he would not let her down, though what he was going to say when he discovered he had rescued the proverbial damsel in distress she could not imagine. She had been going to tell him, but Hassan had intervened and since then she had no real opportunity.

Slipping out of bed, she washed and dressed hurriedly, anxious to complete her toilet before anyone invaded her privacy. No one came, and going to the window, she drew up the blind, careful to keep out of sight of anyone outside. Her room looked out upon a sunken patio at the rear of the house filled with flowers, canna lilies, roses and ordinary herbaceous plants, its enclosing walls covered with the brilliant foam of bougainvillea and purple morning glories.

Téo and Zillah were below her eating an early breakfast in the comparative cool of the hour before sun-up. Neither was dressed. Téo wore a black Moorish robe girded about him with a striped fringed sash which made him look like an oriental despot except for his brown bare head. His lean bronzed cheeks were freshly shaved. Zillah wore a peignoir of gold and scarlet, her luxuriant black hair loose upon her shoulders. The aroma of fresh coffee wafted upwards towards Peta mingled with the garden scents.

Téo was eyeing his companion complacently; he had a sleek relaxed appearance that caused Peta to wonder if they had spent the night together. But in spite of his collection of accommodating friends, he did not give the impression of being a rake. Perhaps his connection with the voluptuous Zillah was legitimate and they were engaged, a supposition Peta found curiously unpalatable.

'Truly you are a little mad, *mon ami*,' the woman was saying. 'Why do you burden yourself with this tiresome youth? Wouldn't it have been more sensible to leave him to his deserts?'

They were speaking in English, possibly so that any listening servant would not understand what they were saying. Zillah's English was as good as Téo's; she must be a cultivated woman.

Peta realised that they were talking about her and she could not resist waiting to hear Téo's reply, for he might be repenting of his rash act and there were policemen in Marrakech if he decided to turn her in.

'He did do me a service,' Téo pointed out, 'and when he looked at me with such desperation in his eyes ... eyes like...' He broke off and shrugged his shoulders. '*Eh bien*, I felt I must give him a chance. I can find work for him at Dar el Bali and it will be interesting to see if a regular life and discipline can make a good citizen out of this young drop-out.'

39

'From what I know of that breed you're wasting your time,' Zillah declared. 'Nor will he thank you for your efforts. You should hand him over to the British Consul.'

'Who, like the Moroccan government, is losing patience with the genus hippy. They're always getting stranded or being caught smuggling. He would probably have been given a stiff sentence, and I'd be surprised if he has any family to be concerned about his fate. The silly creatures have usually cut themselves off from their kindred.'

Peta was conscious of rising anger at this injustice. There were many hard-working students who took their holidays abroad the hard way, being unable to afford any other and who were peaceable and law-abiding. Téo had no right to judge them all by a few unfortunate examples. As for herself, he knew nothing about her circumstances and doubted her statement that she was a student on vacation. Merely because she wore casual clothes and travelled rough he had concluded she was a vagrant. Her impulse was to shout down to them the information that she was a respectable girl training for a profession, her only fault that she had allowed herself to be duped into being a carrier by the cowardice of a one-time friend.

But prudence restrained her; her presence was supposed to be a secret from Zillah's staff and her story might not be believed. If she wanted to cross the Atlas she had better keep quiet, and once established in the oasis she would disclose who and what she was, and if Téo contacted her father he might find a means to get her safely home. She would not own, even to herself, that she was reluctant to declare herself a woman in Zillah's contemptuous presence, with whom she would compare so unfavourably.

For the first time in her active life she regretted that she had neglected to cultivate her feminine charms, then perceiving the drift of her thoughts checked herself fiercely. Did she want to set up in competition with the luscious

Zillah for a man's favours? She was above such degradation. It was merely that she was feeling lonely and cut off from human companionship and the intimacy of the two beneath her was making her feel depressed.

Footsteps stopping outside her door gave her barely time to spring back from the window before it was flung open. She gathered the folds of her d'jellaba about her as a girl came in carrying a tray of coffee and fresh rolls. Peta was surprised to see her, she had thought her presence was unknown, but Madame must have told her servants of the late night arrival of Monsieur d'Argentière's supposed 'cousin'.

The girl was round-faced and bold-eyed, wearing some sort of uniform, and she evidently copied her mistress's manners, for there was no mistaking the come-hither look in her eye.

'*Bon jour, monsieur,*' she said brightly, making play with her eyelashes. '*J'éspère que vous avez bien dormi?*'

'*Oui, merci,*' Peta returned, realising with amusement that the girl was trying to flirt with her. 'I was tired after my long journey.'

'You flew from France?' the girl asked, setting down her tray. 'Ah, *c'est bon* to meet somone French from the old country.'

She clasped her hands and ogled Peta.

Desirous of heading her off the subject of where she had come from, Peta imitated a masculine stance and appraising gaze that she had seen Osric use and told the girl she was a delightful visitor to have first thing in the morning, and what was her name?

'Suzette,' the girl told her, bridling, and her glance went to Peta's tumbled bed. 'Monsieur would like me to stay?'

Peta's French became mixed with English as she hastily expressed her regret that there was no time. Monsieur her cousin would be anxious to take the road as soon as possible. She had barely leisure to swallow her coffee before he

41

would be calling for her.

'A pity,' Suzette sighed. 'You are very handsome, *monsieur*,' and she looked at Peta languishingly.

The compliment, insincere though she felt it to be, had an unexpected effect upon Peta. Suddenly she was filled with triumph; she had been promoted to being an all-conquering male! Yielding to a mischievous impulse, she threw back her hood and swaggered up to the expectant Suzette, taking her by the chin and gazing with pretence ardour into her small black eyes.

'*Charmante*,' she said. 'I only wish I could stay longer, *mon petit chou*.' She sighed regretfully, '*Mais, hélas*, duty calls.'

'You go over the mountains with the formidable Monsieur d'Argentière?' Suzette inquired. '*Vraiment, vous êtes un brave garçon, monsieur.*'

'It is nothing, I'm used to savage lands,' Peta told her loftily. 'Nor do I find Théodore formidable—we are related, you understand.'

It gave her great satisfaction to speak thus familiarly of Téo, which she would never have dared to do to his face.

'But first you will kiss me, yes?' Suzette requested, pouting her lips.

'*Avec plaisir, chérie*,' Peta declared, determined to play her part.

Somewhat gingerly she bent towards the girl.

'Stop that, you young devil!'

Peta jumped violently, outraged that Téo should dare to enter her bedroom without knocking, forgetting he thought she was a boy. She swung round to meet his heavy frown and Suzette scuttled away, giggling.

'Young as you are, I see you've been infected by the permissive morals of your cult,' the cold voice went on, 'but I'll trouble you to leave Madame's maids alone. It's a poor return for her hospitality to seek to seduce her staff.'

Peta stifled a desire to laugh, his misapprehension was so preposterous.

'I'd no intention of harming the girl,' she told him. 'She was making up to me and it would have been rude to snub her.'

'Of course you blame the woman, but I saw what I saw.'

Amusement was swamped by anger, he persisted in mis-judging her. She said rashly:

'Like mistress, like maid. I don't suppose you snubbed Madame's advances.'

'*Nom de dieu*, you impudent young dog!'

She instinctively swerved to avoid the blow which caught her on the side of her face and made her eyes water. Had she met the full force of it, it would have felled her.

'You brute!' she gasped.

She saw puzzlement in his face, for her gesture, hand to smitten cheek, had been wholly feminine. As he met the reproach in her eyes, his became troubled.

'Don't look at me like that,' he almost implored her. Then, hardening, he said sharply, 'You won't always get round me with your limpid grey eyes.'

He had told Zillah her eyes reminded him of someone—someone who must have been dear to him, judging by his reaction. Peta longed to ask who that person was, but knew he would never tell her, not while he believed her to be a precocious youth. She turned away, pulling her hood back over her head. Her cheek stung and her heart was hot with resentment. Zillah had said he could be brutal, and she was right.

'Eat your breakfast,' he said harshly. 'We start in ten minutes,' and abruptly he left the room.

It was Hassan who came to fetch her, after she had forced herself to eat a little and drink the coffee, for after Téo's blow all appetite had left her, but she knew it would be a long time before their next meal. The news of her supposed relationship with Téo must have been broadcast, for he welcomed her with a friendly grin that split his dark face. The Moroccans are a mixed race, but Berbers predominate over the Arab strain in the south. Originally a fair-skinned race, often with light eyes, they have become mixed with the black men from the desert, and Hassan, though he spoke the Berber dialect, betrayed a negroid ancestry. Like most of his countrymen he knew a little French, and he said to her:

'*Allons, monsieur.*'

Concealing the red mark on her cheek by holding her hood over it, Peta followed him. She had no luggage to take with her.

Téo was waiting for them beside the truck. He was wearing for coolness the traditional white Arab headdress with its double cords which suited his aquiline face. He told her curtly to sit in front and she followed Hassan into the cab.

It was early as Téo hoped to leave the heat of the plain before the temperature soared. Zillah, still in her scarlet and gold negligee, but discreetly covered by a long black veil, came out to see them off. Téo kissed her hand, as she said:

'*Prends garde, mon ami.*' Then as he swung himself into the cab. 'May God have you in his keeping.'

Her black eyes were full of tenderness, but Téo's held no response; he was full of impatience to be off as he carelessly reciprocated her blessing.

He was hard, hard as granite, Peta reflected, and wrapped up in his own concerns. She almost pitied Zillah who served him with loving kindness in all ways and was merely used for his convenience.

The widow had thrown Peta a curious glance, but she did not speak to her. Peta would have liked to thank her for her hospitality, but could hardly do so without some acknowledgment of her presence, which except for the one swift look the woman preferred to ignore.

The truck's engine sprang to life under Téo's manipulations, and rumbled out of the cul-de-sac on to the highway and across the red fertile plain towards the foothills some forty miles away. Peta looked back towards the walls of the old city and its distinctive tower and wondered if she would ever see it again. Then her gaze turned to the distant Atlas, its peaks turning all colours in the rays of the new risen sun, beyond which lay adventure.

# CHAPTER THREE

Téo called a halt in a fold of the mountains before tackling the final and steepest part of the ascent of the pass. Their route had been through beautiful scenery amid pine trees, green oaks and oleander, but now the landscape was becoming more barren. He told Peta that the way was called the Kasbah Royal Road, for the country on the other side of the mountains was dotted with a whole chain of Ksour, the plural of Ksar, which meant a fortified Saharan kasbah, and in the old days the inhabitants had need of these mud-walled fortresses as a protection against the fierce desert tribes who so frequently raided them. Peta received the information in unresponsive silence; her cheek still smarted, but little by little her resentment was forgotten. She was posing as a boy and she had definitely been impudent, so she could expect no less. She amused herself by cogitating how Téo would have introduced her to Zillah if he had known she was a girl, but then he would never have taken her to the house at all, he would have dumped her at the first mission they came across, and there were European missionaries here and there, when no doubt she would have been exhorted to repent her sins and turned over to the authorities to expiate them. Dar el Bali, even if it turned out to be as hot as hell and her arrival there was full of problems, was preferable to such a fate, and she must preserve her disguise until she reached it. Téo had no suspicion that she was not what she seemed, her shirt and jeans hung upon her loosely, she had become thinner since she came to Africa, and she clung to the concealing folds of her d'jellaba. He never looked at her closely, fearing to be confronted by the resemblance that so distressed him.

Now she had been acknowledged as a member of the party, Téo had no qualms about making use of her. They stopped outside a village for their midday rest and he ordered her to go foraging for provisions.

'Hassan is a creature of habit and needs his siesta,' he told her. 'So you can do something for your living. Here, take this,' he handed her some money. 'The villagers will be ready to barter anything for cash.'

'But can I make myself understood?' she asked doubtfully.

He shrugged carelessly. 'Most of them knew a few French or English words, this is becoming a tourist route nowadays. Use your wits, boy, you must have had to recourse to them often enough before.'

She hated the scornful note that came into his voice whenever he referred to her former activities, and she started off determined to show him that she was more than capable of performing such a simple errand. He called her back.

'A word of warning—don't try to make passes at any of the native girls or you may get your throat cut. These Berbers are jealous of their women's honour.'

He laughed at her outraged expression and she ran off with burning cheeks. One good thing about the episode with Suzette, it had confirmed his belief in her masculinity, though she fiercely resented his jeering attitude towards it. He took his fun where he could find it, so why should not she, if she had been the youth he imagined?

She returned with the cooked meat, flat bread and other items that he had suggested, having obtained them without difficulty. The villagers were used to serving wayfarers. She had also procured several bottles of Coca-Cola.

'Which was the only liquid they seemed to have except goats' milk,' she said apologetically, 'and I'd nothing to put that in.'

'It'll do, at least it's wet. You'll find that stuff everywhere between the North Pole and Timbuktu.'

They ate their meal in the shade of the trees by the side of a mountain stream. A bus came lumbering up the pass, and Peta was told that they ran daily from Marrakech when the pass was open and even in winter snow ploughs endeavoured to keep it clear. After they had eaten, Hassan fell asleep again and so did Téo, but Peta felt no inclination to do so. She sat crosslegged watching the Frenchman's unconscious face. He slept quietly, though Hassan snored, and she waved the encroaching flies away with a piece of fern. She wondered how old he was; about thirty, she supposed, at the height of his vigorous strength, yet old enough to have suffered, for there must be some tragedy in his past connected with the person whose eyes were like her own. A woman, presumably—wife, mother or sweetheart? Would he ever tell her?

Suddenly his eyes flickered open and he met her gaze. He smiled and his whole face softened as if he beheld a much loved image. Then full consciousness returned to him, his smile vanished and he hastily looked away from her, springing to his feet with a swift lithe movement. Glancing at his watch, he said:

'I hope to make Ouarzazate by tonight and Dar el Bali tomorrow. I make this trip about once in three months, not only to collect stores but to report to the authorities in Casablanca.' He spoke in a curt clipped tone as if he were anxious to obliterate that moment of softness.

'You have another friend in Ouarzazate?' she asked, wondering about accommodation.

'Yes, Sheik Omar, and Hassan has relations living there. As my cousin you'll have to come with me, though by rights your place is with him.'

Glancing at the sleeping Hassan, she exclaimed involuntarily:

'Oh no!'

He raised his eyebrows. 'Hassan's a decent fellow.'

'It ... it isn't that, but I'm not used to native households.'

'Bit of a cissy, aren't you?' A quick glance, and his eyes slid away from her. 'But you're very young, so perhaps you can be redeemed by hard work and clean living.'

Peta said nothing, though she was incensed by his assumption that she was a ne'er-do-well and work-shy, and the vague suggestion of rehabilitating her. Téo was in for a surprise when he discovered her sex, but she was determined that he should not do so until they reached their destination, when it would be too late for him to leave her by the wayside; she hoped very much he might find her something to do in his village, clerical work perhaps, for she did not want to have to leave him. He attracted her, she liked the long lean lines of his body that showed both grace and energy, also his clean-cut features and the strong lines of jaw and chin, the direct gaze of his tawny eyes, but more than his outward seeming, she was intrigued by what lay beneath his assured exterior. He was a mature man of courage and integrity whose experience of life far exceeded her own, an intelligent man who chose to bury himself on the edge of the desert to serve an alien people who would not hesitate to dispense with him if his services were no longer required.

Wanting to know what she might expect to find there, she began to question him about the oasis that seemed to so enchant him.

'It's a *palmerie*, as they call them on the far side of the Anti Atlas,' he told her, 'and on the fringe of the Sahara, a Godforsaken, thirsty land. But there is rich mineral wealth in these mountains. Manganese is mined on the futher side of this pass, and phosphates are found in the west, but that

49

is only a fraction of what is waiting to be discovered. It is part of my job to look for it.'

A far-away look came into his eyes, and she divined that though he might call the country Godforsaken, he was fascinated by it.

'Is there any uranium?' she asked, for she knew that was the goal of every prospector who sought for it as eagerly as men had once hunted for gold.

He shrugged his shoulders. 'Maybe, but I haven't struck any yet. But that isn't my only job. I supervise the irrigation system at Dar el Bali—a river flows down to the village into a reservoir we've built to preserve the water during the dry season, that is to be enlarged. It provides work for the villagers who own precious little besides their date palms and they are being attacked by a disease that so far aerial spraying has failed to check. It is hoped that with more water they can grow more grain to feed themselves and their flocks.'

'You have the welfare of this village very much at heart,' Peta suggested softly.

Again the expressive Gallic shrug. 'It is a good place for a man to learn to forget.'

A shadow crossed his face and he stared into the distance as if it were peopled by ghosts. Peta gazed at him with her eyes full of compassion and turning his head he met her wide sympathetic eyes.

'Don't look at me like that,' he told her harshly.

Peta hastily turned away, saddened by this rebuff. Anxious to divert him, and reminded by the wide spaces on either side of her that but for him she would be confined to a cell in Casa or Rabat awaiting trial instead of enjoying her liberty in the sun and air, she said with a rush of thankfulness:

'I really am intensely grateful to you, Monsieur d'Argentière.'

'It's too soon to thank me, *mon enfant*, you don't know what you're in for. Oh, you'll be safe enough at Dar el Bali, but you won't appreciate its lack of amenities. There's no Hotel du Sud there like the Tourist Board has built in so many places even as far out as Zagora—it's stark.'

'You won't frighten me off,' she told him eagerly. 'I want to see it, my father says the Anti Atlas is a strange land ...' and she stopped abruptly.

'Your father knows it?' he rapped, staring at her.

'He ... he's read about it,' she amended hastily. 'And so have I. I know there is the Moyen Atlas, the Haut Atlas and then the Anti Atlas, which is composed of old black hills belonging to an earlier age....' She again broke off as she met his quizzical expression.

'Quite the little geologist,' he said sarcastically, 'and where did you learn so much about the Atlas terrain?'

'At school.'

'I didn't know your sort ever stayed long enough at school to learn anything,' he said cruelly, 'and by the look of you, you should still be there.'

About to tell him she was attending college, Peta checked herself. She had already told him she was a student, which he disbelieved. He probably thought she was younger than she was and to reveal her actual age was risky. Lads of nineteen were almost men. He took her flush of anger for guilt and smiled benignly.

'I bet you were adept at playing truant. I wonder if you young reprobates ever stop to think of the men who fought to provide the universal education which you can't appreciate.'

Again she checked a furious retort. She was far from despising the facilities offered to her, in fact she had utilised them, but the less she said about herself the better if she wanted to cross the Haut Atlas with him.

'*Eh bien*,' he went on more kindly, viewing her downcast

51

face shadowed by her hood. 'It's never too late to mend, and perhaps I can teach you to do something useful.' He again glanced at his watch. 'It's more than time we were off, this log seems to intend to sleep until night fall.'

He nudged Hassan with his foot, and the man stirred, grumbled, and finally sat up rubbing his eyes.

'*En avant*,' said his master, and walked to the truck.

The last part of the journey up the pass was a long gruelling climb, the road winding round a continuous series of hairpin bends, with precipitous declivities on either side, while stupendous views opened below them. Several times Téo had to stop the truck to cool the engine, and they seemed to be poised between earth and sky upon narrow ledges of rock with infinity above and below.

'Now I know what a fly on the ceiling feels like,' Peta said on one of these occasions.

'Scared?' Téo demanded.

'N-o, only tremendously impressed.'

'There's hope for you yet,' he remarked enigmatically.

The sun was sinking as the top of the eight-thousand-odd-feet-high Tizi N' Tichka was reached, its rays piercing the gaps and gorges in the scoured rocks, bathing their fantastic shapes in a bath of blood. The air was cool and sweet, but the few storm-twisted trees and the contorted boulders indicated how the suffocating simoom coming straight from the Sahara could ravage these summits when it blew.

'Now you've entered another world,' Téo told Peta as the truck began to descend the long southern slopes of the mountains. The land formation changed entirely. During the earlier part of their upward climb they had traversed country almost Alpine in character, but the side exposed to the desert winds was stony and arid. Long rows of serrated rock ran for miles along the ridges above the huddled flat-roofed native villages. Cultivation there was in sheltered places, terraces planted with maize and barley, and the villages were terraced also, but the overall aspect was brown and bleak.

Peta had complete confidence in Téo's driving, however awesome the road. As she sat between him and Hassan her eyes watched his strong competent brown hands upon the wheel. Long-fingered shapely hands. She became very conscious of his proximity, but the sensation did not displease her. She would have liked to go on for ever through this fantastic world seated beside him without past or future in a kind of sensuous dream.

Down they went until they came to the flat barren expanses leading to the Sahara, flushed to carmine, vermilion scarlet and magenta by the farewell kiss of the sun, the dusty earth, buildings, rocks, gorges and dried watercourses washed by a crimson tide. Vegetation only lurked in hidden indentations in the parched ground, without river or lake.

The lights were coming on in Ouarzazate as they approached the little town, which was one of the last outposts of civilisation and comfort before the rigours of the desert began. It lay along the banks of a river, now a mere trickle of ooze amidst groves of dusty palms. Although it boasted several hotels, Téo preferred to call upon his Berber friend, who with the hospitality of his countrymen insisted that he should do so whenever he was passing through.

Hassan dropped them in the middle of the town and went off with the truck, which was to be parked in his kinfolk's yard. Téo bade Peta follow him and led the way down a narrow street between the high walls of native houses, windowless on the side exposed to view.

'The Dutchman leaves his curtains undrawn so that the passer-by can admire his possessions,' he remarked, 'the British keep their windows covered, but the Arabs and Berbers surround their homes with high walls to preserve their privacy. I bet you've never been in a real Moroccan home, Pierre, it'll be an experience for you.'

Peta stopped. 'But, *monsieur*, I . . . I'll be an imposition,' she protested. 'They don't know me, they won't be expecting me.'

'The Sheikh would welcome any friend of mine, his hospitality is boundless and you're supposed to be my cousin from France, so will be doubly so. Incidentally, I *have* got cousins in France, though they're not called Brun. Come along, Pierre, where else can you go?' He became impatient as she still hung back. 'You're being tiresome and I'm hungry. Aren't you?'

So perforce she had no choice but to go with him into the house.

Sheikh Omar ben Ibrahim adhered to the old Moroccan traditions; though among the younger generation wives greeted guests together with their husbands, Omar's women remained invisible to males. Lady visitors joined them in their own quarters while their escorts were entertained by their host.

The house to which Téo conducted Peta was also old-fashioned in construction. A stout wooden door bound with iron was set in the thick windowless walls, looking more like the entrance to a prison than a residence. Téo hammered upon it with the metal knocker, and it was opened by an old man in a striped d'jellaba wearing a turban. He recognised the Frenchman at once and salaamed, exclaiming joyfully, 'El Sidi!' followed by words of greeting.

He ushered them along a dark passage through the thickness of the walls that merged into a corridor running the length of the house. This ended in a stone patio containing a well-head, several palm trees and a few fig trees. Around it the rooms of the house were grouped.

Before they reached it he turned aside and led them into the main reception room, which was also the dining room, a high-ceilinged apartment with whitewashed walls and a long bench covered with cushions along one side of it. The mosaic floor showed through between handsome handwoven rugs. The ceiling was of carved wood, and the upper half of the walls were ornamented with patterns in coloured tiles and stucco. There was one picture, a portrait of the reigning Sultan. Although the hotels had electricity there was none in this house. Two ornate metal holders hung from the ceiling on long chains, each holding a brass oil lamp. The light they gave was subdued and mellow. The guide made another obeisance and withdrew leaving them alone.

'It's like a scene from the Arabian Nights,' Peta murmured, awestruck. 'Is it real?'

'Definitely, and functional—you're seeing the interior of a typical Berber house unchanged for centuries. Nothing did change in Morocco for hundreds of years until this century. Now, *hélas*, modernisation is laying its mediocre blight over the country, but here and there you'll still find a pocket of resistance to innovations like this place.' Téo looked round appreciatively.

Peta did not share his regret for the passing of the old order. At that moment she would have welcomed the installation of modern plumbing. She desperately needed a bath and it seemed unlikely she would find even adequate washing facilities.

The Sheikh came in to welcome them, a hawk-nosed grey bearded man wearing a turban and white robes. His dark sunken eyes lit up at the sight of Téo.

'*Salaam-O-aleikum*, peace be unto you,' he greeted him in a deep resonant voice. He touched his breast, then Téo's, and his own again. They conversed together in Arabic and then Téo presented Peta. She did not know quite what was expected of her, so bowed from her waist. Omar regarded her for a moment with his piercing gaze and she was thankful for the dim lighting in the room. Then he repeated his greeting wishing her peace.

'I regard your kinsman almost as a blood brother,' he

told her in French. 'Any relative of his is doubly welcome.'

Peta hung her head, feeling a fraud, and her meek attitude seemed to please him, for he murmured something to Téo about the deference due to age and experience which modern youth even in his country seemed to be forgetting.

'Pierre knows his place,' Téo returned, giving her a mischievous glance.

A servant was summoned, not the old doorkeepr but a mere lad with a face as beardless as Peta's, and he was commanded to take them to the guest room.

'For a wash and brush up,' Téo whispered to her as they left the presence chamber. He had brought with him a canvas bag containing a few necessities for the night which he had handed over to the doorkeeper. Peta had nothing, not even a toothbrush. The boy led them out into the patio and into another room that had access to it in which a boat-shaped lamp gave a faint illumination. It was furnished with a divan bed and several tables and stools. On one of the tables was a copper bowl and a steaming can of water. The boy pointed to the bed beside which Téo's bag was placed and made some observation, to which Téo nodded and he withdrew.

'He'll have a camp bed brought in for you,' Téo told her.

Peta quailed. Although she had been anxious about the night's accommodation she had not realised she would have to share with him. Luckily the light was too dim for him to perceive her perturbation.

'The *cabinet de toilette* is across the patio behind a lattice screen,' he told her. 'Primitive but adequate.'

With an embarrassed murmur Peta escaped into the open air, hoping she would not meet anyone. The patio seemed deserted; above its high walls was a black velvet sky spangled with stars, the fresh night air cooled her flushed cheeks and her momentary panic died away. With a little ingenuity she should be able to avoid detection, but she would have to appear at supper with the Sheikh amid an all-male company. To feign illness would draw undesired attention to herself, and to insist that she did not require food would offend Moroccan hospitality, so there was no way in which she could evade it.

Peta was not lacking in courage, but she dreaded discovery which would constitute an abuse of the very hospitality she was so anxious not to wound. It was too late to confess to Téo now, it would put him in a most awkward position. She would simply have to go through with it and trust to luck—and the dim lighting—to maintain her disguise.

She came back to find Téo naked to the waist and towelling his brown torso.

'You have been a time,' he complained. 'You will only have time to wash your hands and face. Take off your d'jellaba and shoes. Ali has brought you a pair of babouches.'

'Thank you very much,' she murmured, reluctantly removing her gown. Her jeans and shirt were loose-fitting, and she kept the latter fastened up to her throat, about which a silk handkerchief was knotted. She loosened it and arranged it to hang over the very slight swell of her figure. She slipped off her dusty sandals, leather ones with thick soles, a serviceable pair she had bought for hiking. The babouches, the heelless native slippers, were too big for her and not easy to walk in even when they fitted. About to make a remark about Cinderella losing her shoe, she checked herself. Much wiser not to identify herself with anyone feminine.

'I'm afraid I've no spare clothing to lend you, you'll have to sleep raw,' Téo remarked cheerfully. 'At least you won't need to borrow my razor. About time your beard began to sprout, isn't it?'

She flashed him a nervous look under her eyelashes, but he was engaged in pulling on his shirt.

'I must be a late developer,' she said vaguely.

He laughed. 'Not you! You're a most precocious little beast from what I've seen of you.'

He was recalling Suzette. Peta asked hastily to divert him:

'Are there no women here?'

'Plenty, but they have their own quarters. Oh, Omar doesn't keep a harem, if that's what you're thinking. Most Moslems are monogamous nowadays, but in addition to his wife, he supports all his female dependants. Sometimes they may include a widowed mother, unmarried sisters, daughters and daughters-in-law, though in his case I don't know what his family comprises. It isn't done to speak of his womenfolk.'

'Isn't he awfully old-fashioned? I mean, on our travels women were very much in evidence in the markets and cafés even as landladies.'

'They weren't in the Sheikh's class, *mon garçon*. Yes, he does cling to traditions, but a lot of them still do, especially in the country. *Eh bien*, we had better go and join him.'

The men had assembled when Peta and Téo reached the dining room, and there were more formal greetings. They included Omar's eldest son, an uncle visiting the family and an assortment of grandsons. The younger men wore European suits, the more juvenile of the boys jeans and shirts, and to Peta's relief looked very like herself, with their brown faces and black hair, except that their heads were covered by either a fez or a cap. Téo was given the place of honour next to the Sheikh and Peta was seated on his other side on the bench along the wall. Then some women did appear, but whether they were family or merely servants, Peta could not discover. They brought in low tables which they set before the men. Then followed the washing of hands. Peta knew enough to hold out her fingers for the water to be poured over them and accepted the towel from Téo which after use she handed to her neighbour. The women were swathed in black drapery, the orthodox dress of the Moslem similar to the white haiks Peta had seen in the north, only of more sombre hue. Peta felt a fraud being waited upon by them, and was nervous of their keener perceptions, but they kept their eyes downcast as was expected of modest females, never raising them beyond her long slim legs.

The communal dishes covered by ornate conical lids were placed upon the tables and they were each served with a round of bread that would serve as a plate. Then their host evoked the blessing of Allah upon the food and the covers were removed. The dish was a concoction of mutton and rice with many spices and garnishes. The partakers extracted pieces of savoury meat with their fingers and mopped up the gravy with pieces of their bread. The roast was followed by the inevitable couscous, the foundation of which was semolina and could be either savoury or sweet, though this was the former. The expert rolled the stuff into little balls, dipped it into a sauce and swallowed it. As this operation required practice, Peta was grateful for the offer of a spoon. The meal concluded with sweetmeats composed of honey, almonds and other nuts. Then the hands were again washed in the proffered copper bowls, the tables removed, and the master of the house proceeded to make the mint tea. As was customary no drink had been provided with the food.

The utensils were spread before the Sheikh, a steaming kettle on a little charcoal brazier, the teapot, boxes of green tea and sugar, and the glasses. When the brew was finally made to the mixer's satisfaction, he poured it into the glasses which were given to each guest.

'And you must drink three glasses,' Téo whispered to Peta in English, 'or they'll be offended.'

Peta had a vision of her mother presiding over the afternoon tea-table at home, the silver teapot and china cups and saucers. It was not only in Morocco that tea-making was a ritual. She had to repress an almost irresistible desire to giggle as she pictured the conventional Maud's consternation if she could see her daughter now, imbibing the beverage amidst an assembly of dark-skinned men.

But she was very weary and had to pinch herself to keep awake. At last Téo noticed her fatigue, and took pity upon her.

'My young cousin needs his bed,' he said apologetically to Omar. 'He is unused to Moroccan ways and he has had a long hard journey. May he be excused?'

The Sheikh nodded his head and addressed some remark to her that she did not understand and deputed a boy, probably a grandson, to escort her to her room. Peta stood up, bowed to her host and to the rest of the company and followed him. He carried a small lamp to light their way across the courtyard, and when they reached the bedroom, she saw a narrow camp bed had been installed alongside Téo's divan. The boy put down the lamp, gave her a wide grin and a wink, and retreated silently into the night, leaving her staring down at it.

The first thing to do was to remove it as far as possible from Téo's resting place, which she accomplished with some difficulty, for though not heavy it showed a tendency to collapse. Mercifully he was still gossiping with his host, and she would have time to get into bed and be asleep before he came. After some hesitation she decided to undress, though there was no clean robe for her use tonight. She folded her jeans and shirt, putting them on a stool, and wrapped herself in one of the soft blankets that lay on the bed, trusting that she would wake before Téo in the morning. She left the lamp alight on the table beside his bed, glad to see that its faint illumination did not reach her corner.

In spite of her tiredness she lay awake for a long time, listening to the sounds coming from the house, a baby's wail, a cat's mew, and from the main room music, a wild plaintive air played upon a reed flute. Evidently Omar was providing entertainment for his guest. She did not feel very pleased with Téo for exposing her to this ordeal. though how great a one it had been he was unaware, but she had to admit that she could hardly expect him to alter his usual routine for the sake of a truant he had picked up en route. Though he was French, there seemed to be a strong affinity between him and these mountain men; he even looked like them. He also had very much the Muslim attitude towards women, which would cause him to view her escapade as all the more reprehensible. She smiled to herself in the darkness. Théodore d'Argentière was going to have the surprise of his life when they arrived at Dar el Bali, for she would have to confess her sex eventually, and it would be rather fun to witness his astonished chagrin when he learned how she had duped him. At long last she drifted into sleep, reflecting that as Téo was so late, he would not be awake when she rose in the morning.

Unfortunately it was she who overslept. She woke to a dash of cold water on her face and looked up spluttering to behold a naked Téo, except for a towel folded about his middle, standing over her an empty water jar in his hand.

'Wake up, you lazy little devil,' he commanded her. 'Come into the patio and I'll sluice you down with well water, there's no one about and it's time you had a bath.'

From his dripping hair he had obviously used the treatment on himself.

'But the women——' Peta gasped, sitting up and hugging a blanket round her.

'Have their own court, of course. They don't intrude here.'

Information that did not reassure her.

'I ... I can't stand cold water,' she faltered, 'my heart ...'

For a moment she thought he was going to strip away the concealing bedclothes, and the organ she had libelled as being weak seemed to stand still. He would be overcome with embarrassment if he did so, and so would she. Moreover, Sheikh Omar would be horrified if he discovered how he had been deceived; he would never forgive such a breach of decorum. Meanwhile Téo stood above her like an avenging god, and in spite of her panic, her eyes registered the slim perfection of his body, broad-shouldered, narrow-hipped, the skin smooth and brown over his rippling muscles. Deep down in the centre of her being something stirred, the birth of her latent femininity.

To her relief, Téo turned away, muttering, 'Scruffy little beast,' and when she dared to look again he had put on his trousers and was drawing on his shirt.

'*Dépêchez-vous*,' he said impatiently. 'We must make an early start. I only hope Hassan's brought the truck round. I'll go and see before I shave.'

He thrust his feet into his shoes and hurried out of the room. Peta dressed with lightning speed, anxious to be covered by her d'jellaba by the time he returned. She went out into the patio and drew up a bucket of water from the well, in which she laved her face and hands. When Téo eventually did return carrying a bowl of hot water she was folding the blankets on her bed.

'Leave that for the women to do,' he told her. 'You'll find some coffee in the main room if you want some. I want to make Dar el Bali by noon.'

At that early hour the interior of the house was dim and cool, not that it ever became very hot. The small narrow windows did not admit the sun and the thick walls kept out

62

the heat. Peta with her robe draped about her was able to make her farewells with confidence.

Perhaps it was ungracious, but she had never been more thankful to leave any place than she was to quit the hospitable roof of Sheikh Omar ibn Ibrahim.

# CHAPTER FOUR

THE road threaded its way through the valleys of the Anti Atlas, a torrid sun-blistered country of rock and sand. Téo left the main road, taking an unsurfaced track below a cliff of huddled boulders that looked as if they might topple at any moment. The way was called a *piste* in that locality. It came out on a ridge from which they could see depressions and oases spreading towards an illimitable distance that was the Sahara. Directly below them was a patch of green and the glint of water, and Téo said: 'Dar el Bali.'

The landscape on either side had a lunar aspect, incapable of supporting life, and that little patch of green was a welcome sight, but the descent to it down a succession of hairpin bends proved it was much further away than it looked; distances were deceptive in that dry clear air. When at last they reached the valley floor, Téo pointed to a cleft in the cliff behind them through which a thin stream trickled.

'Our lifeline,' he told her. 'The *oued* shrinks to nothing as the summer advances, but in winter it is fed by melting snows to a torrent. Sometimes this road is swept away by a flash flood. We have trapped the water at the *palmerie* in a reservoir. Most of the rivers on this side of the Atlas lose themselves in the desert where they are sucked dry.'

Peta murmured some sort of assent; she was too anxious about what was going to happen upon her arrival to care what became of the *oueds*. Unaware of her preoccupation and its cause, Téo continued to instruct her.

'There's plenty of water under the Sahara, but to pump it up to the surface would be astronomically expensive.

However, as expansion becomes more necessary on this overcrowded planet, perhaps a time will come when we shall have to try to reclaim it. Meanwhile the sand is encroaching upon the south of the desert and nobody has the resources to try to stem its advance.'

The road had become paved when they approached the village. 'Some of my work,' Téo told her, smiling, and they entered a world of waving date palms and even grass growing on the banked-up sides of the artificial lake. There were clusters of flat-roofed mud houses between which ran irrigation ditches, mud being the principal building material in that locality. At one end was the kasbah, the home of the Caid, which boasted two quite pretentious towers. Peta glanced at it without interest; she had seen a great many kasbahs while crossing the Atlas, large, small and half ruined. At the opposite side of the reservoir to the Caid's dwelling was a white stone-built house with a few tattered rose bushes in front of it, enclosed by a fence to keep out the donkeys and goats which wandered at will.

'My home,' Téo told her. 'It was originally an army post used by the French forces, but now they've gone and the Caid, preferring his kasbah, rents it to me.'

Behind the house was a paved courtyard that had once been a parade ground, bounded by a row of storage sheds and outbuildings.

The truck halted in the yard and several Berber men appeared to help with the unloading. Téo leaped out of the cab, and Peta nervously followed Hassan out on the other side.

'Now then, young Pierre,' Téo said to her, 'you can start to earn your keep. All the articles in the truck have to be transferred into the sheds and you can lend my boys a hand, while I go to see what Ismael has to report to me.'

He strode away into the house, leaving Peta to glance apprehensively at Hassan. He let down the tailboard and began to heave the sacks towards the waiting men. They weighed about a hundredweight and were too heavy for Peta to lift, but there were various smaller bundles and parcels which the men, with a contemptuous consideration for her frail physique, signed to her to carry. Nothing was very light and her back and arms were aching by the time the load was housed, and sweat ran down her spine and sides, making her shirt stick to her uncomfortably under her d'jellaba which she had tucked up about her waist, using a piece of cord as a belt. She was glad of the protection of its hood against the fierce rays of the sun.

The unloading completed, she stood dejectedly in the shadow of the truck, longing for something to drink. A mechanical pump, the machine Téo had fetched from the docks at Casablanca, was beside her in the yard. Téo came back and began to examine it. Looking up at her, he inquired:

'Not any sort of a mechanic, are you, Pierre?'

'I'm afraid I don't know anything about machinery,' she replied.

'It would have been phenomenal luck if you did.' He regarded her from under frowning brows. 'Fairly useless sort of a specimen, aren't you? We'll put you on to digging irrigation trenches, that should develop your muscles and doesn't require any skill.'

He became oblivious of her, absorbed in fiddling with his machine. The folds of his headdress obscured his face and he seemed quite impervious to the blistering heat of the sun.

Peta said desperately. 'Please, *monsieur*, where am I to lodge, and I should like a wash and a drink, I'm almost dying of thirst.'

'That's a chronic state of being about here,' he told her unsympathetically. 'I'll have to put you up in the house to support the cousin myth. Ismael will see about a room for you later.' She sighed with relief to learn that she would have her own room. 'Meanwhile I can see you definitely need a wash, and so does that garment you persist in wrapping round you. We must find you a pair of shorts which are the most suitable wear about here. Hassan will show you where the stand pipe is and help you to sluice down.'

'No, please,' she cried urgently as he looked round for his man. 'I ... I can manage if you tell me where it is.'

Téo bent his brows upon her in a frown. 'I hope you've no superior notions about your status,' he said sternly. 'We're all equal here.'

'It ... it isn't that ...'

'Ah, I remember, your heart is allergic to cold water, but no water is really cold here without ice. I'll stand for no namby-pamby nonsense Pierre. We won't bother Hassan, I'll strip you myself.'

He took a stride towards her and ripped the d'jellaba from her shoulders, throwing it to the ground. His hands were upon the neck of her shirt, tearing away the flimsy handkerchief, when she put up hers to stay him, the shamed carmine staining her cheeks.

'*Monsieur*, no, please don't!'

'Why not? You make as much fuss as if you have some deformity to hide. Have you?'

His eyes bored down into hers, his hands on the neck of her shirt ready to rend it apart and reveal all she had tried so hard to hide.

'No, *monsieur*, but ...' She turned her head away and said flatly, 'I'm a girl.'

'What?' He started back as if he had touched a snake.

She bowed her head, her arms crossed over her chest; look and gesture were wholly feminine.

'*Mon dieu!*' Téo ejaculated. He picked up the discarded d'jellaba and threw it around her as if he had actually stripped her. Then seizing her arm, he marched her into the

67

house away from any curious eyes that might be watching them.

The front door was open, admitting them to a stone-floored passage way, and he opened another door to one side and pushed her into what was obviously his living room. Its furniture was purely functional, a desk covered with papers, books piled on shelves, a table, and several upright chairs, its only concession to comfort two shabby armchairs covered in leather. It contained a fireplace stacked with tamarisk wood, a reminder that the desert nights could be cold.

Once inside and the door closed he released his hold of her arm, and again sweeping off the d'jellaba studied her from head to foot, grim-lipped.

Now the moment of confrontation had come, Peta no longer felt nervous, and she threw up her head defiantly. She knew she looked and was dirty and unkempt, but how else could she appear after the dusty journey and the time spent toiling in the hot sun carrying his purchases? She had tried to do her part as well as she was able, and he should respect her for that. He had never questioned her sex, so she could not be entirely blamed for his misapprehension.

'*Nom d'un chien*, but you are assuredly a woman,' he said at last. 'How could I have been so blind?'

'You accepted me as a boy, so you never saw me as anything else,' she pointed out. 'That is if you ever looked at me with a seeing eye, which I doubt.'

The feminine pique in her last phrase caused an unwilling smile to curve Téo's mobile lips.

'A characteristically feminine remark,' he commented. 'But, *ciel*, what were your people thinking about to allow you to run round Africa with a gang of hippies?'

'I didn't have to ask their permission, and we weren't hippies,' she returned hotly. 'I keep telling you we're students trying to see the country in our own way.'

68

'Which soon landed you into trouble, but you say "we". Where are your companions, and why did they leave you in the lurch?'

This was Peta's first opportunity to give him a full account of what had befallen her since landing in Morocco. He had indicated by a gesture that she should sit and she sank gratefully into one of the arm chairs. Téo preferred to stand, hands in trouser pockets, supported by the edge of the table. He listened to her recital without interruption, his eyes fixed upon her face watching the swift play of expression cross her sensitive features. He did not doubt her sincerity, but deplored her lack of wisdom.

'This isn't England, or even Europe,' he told her when she had concluded her story. 'For a trip out here you should have chosen your companions with more care. Nice set of scoundrels you seem to have imported! Obviously this Osric became entangled with a smuggling racket. The perpetrators are always on the outlook for greenhorns to use as carriers. Are you in love with him?'

He shot the question at her so abruptly that her eyes widened in surprise.

'Osric? No, of course not. Actually he did make a pass at me, but I found his attentions tiresome.'

'Aha, so he paid you attention, but if his interest was not reciprocated, why did you consent to act as his stooge?'

'I didn't! I told you he put the contraband in my pack when he thought he was going to be caught out. I was quite unsuspecting. I suppose he panicked.'

'Charming character to hide behind a girl, but he was probably smoking kif. That debases a man.'

'Oh no!' But remembering Osric's choice of companions and his nights spent in Fez she feared it might be true.

'And your other friends, were they involved in this?'

'Val was Osric's shadow, so I suppose he was, but I'm sure Keith had nothing to do with it. He was my real pal.'

'Yet he abandoned you.'

'Not really. He wasn't bound to me in any way and he knew I could look after myself under normal circumstances. He didn't know what Osric was doing. We shall link up again when he gets back to England.'

She did not know why she said that, for she did not expect to contact Keith again, nor that he would write. Subconsciously she wanted to show this arrogant man that she had a respectable admirer.

'*Eh bien*, he won't be any help to you in your present predicament,' Téo remarked. He scratched his head. 'What the deuce am I going to do with you?'

'If you'd just let me stay here for a while,' Peta suggested tentatively, 'while we ... er ... think. I won't get in your way and I could perhaps be useful. Help with the ... er ... housework.'

He laughed. 'There are no women in my household. We live rough.'

'Haven't I shown that I can take it?' she demanded.

'You have, but then you were scared to death of being caught. But you must have known you couldn't keep up this farce indefinitely, and Dar el Bali is not a suitable place for a woman.'

'But aren't there women in the village?'

'Natives and born to it. It's different for you, Pierre ... by the way, what's your real name?'

'That—Peta, only it's spelt with an A, not ER.'

'So you didn't lie about that.'

'I haven't actually lied about anything.'

'You have by implication.'

'No favourable opportunity presented itself to correct your mistake, except in the truck, and then I was too frightened to think of anything but escape. I couldn't admit to being a girl with Hassan around and at Madame Sancé's

70

you were otherwise engaged.'

'I'm surprised Zillah didn't spot your sex,' he said wonderingly.

'She had eyes only for you,' Peta returned.

He shot her an ironical glance and she turned her head away, fearful that she had betrayed her jealousy of the other woman. Jealousy? She could not be resenting Zillah's place in his regard, or did she?

Téo began to laugh with genuine amusement as he recalled how he had surprised her with Suzette.

'You were a little minx playing up to that silly girl,' he remarked. He sobered suddenly. 'I struck you.'

'You did.' Involuntarily Peta touched her cheek.

'*Alors*, for that I am truly sorry.'

'You're forgiven,' she said magnanimously. 'Perhaps your penitence could be in the form of a drink? I ... I'm terribly thirsty.'

Talking had aggravated the dryness of her throat and her voice was almost a croak.

'*Mon dieu*, and you unloaded all those parcels! I will say you have, what do you call it, grit, *mon enfant*. But *restes ici*, I will fetch you something. You must forgive my neglect—you have, as one might say, exploded a bombshell.'

He strode out of the room, leaving her to reflect that he had taken her revelation remarkably well, with the result that he was now waiting upon her. That was because he was French, an Arab or a Berber would not so demean himself, but a native would have had a woman in the house to perform such services; apparently he had a man to do the domestic chores. She could not imagine Téo washing up.

He was gone some time and in his absence she continued to gaze curiously about the room, seeking clues to his personality. A silver-mounted frame on the desk with its back towards her attracted her attention. With her ears alert for the sound of Téo's footsteps, she rose to her feet and went

71

to look at it. It was the coloured photograph of a very lovely woman with wide grey eyes that looked directly out of the picture with an appealing gaze. Peta recognized that they were eyes very like her own. Across the bottom was written in a sprawling hand:

*A Téo, coeur de mon coeur.* Lucie.

Peta went back to her seat with a feeling of trespass. She understood now why certain expressions of her own had such an effect upon Téo; she reminded him of the girl in the photograph—Lucie. A soft, feminine-sounding name, which if she lived up to it meant that in all other ways she must be totally different from the boyish Peta Cartwright, the kind of clinging young woman who would appeal to the hard-bitten Téo. That she did appeal was obvious since a chance likeness could make him vulnerable to Peta's distress. But who was she, wife, fiancée or friend? That there was some obstacle between them seemed probable, to account for the look of pain with which Téo recalled her, but whoever she was they must be in love. 'Heart of my heart' was hardly a casual expression of affection. Yet whatever his connection with her was or had been it did not include fidelity, as the episode with Zillah illustrated, but she was apparently far away, and a virile man in a hot country needed relaxation, as her permissive acquaintances would heartily endorse, or perhaps he sought other diversions to forget. Hadn't he said Dar el Bali was a place in which to do just that? It was possible she might be dead. Peta found she was deeply intrigued by Téo's romance, though it could not possibly affect herself in any way. She sensed that whatever he felt for the lady in the silver frame was a much deeper and finer emotion than any sensual urge, and unaccountably the thought depressed her.

Téo returned carrying a tall glass of lemonade which he presented to her.

'The best I have to offer,' he told her, 'at least it's a

change from Coca-Cola, unless you'd like a whisky and soda? I keep some for my own benefit under lock and key so as not to tempt the sons of Islam. Sorry there's no ice.'

'This is lovely, just what I wanted,' Peta said gratefully, sipping the drink which was cool but not cold.

'Don't ever be tempted to drink the water here unless it has been boiled.'

'I do know better than that,' she said a little resentfully.

'*Eh bien*, it's a point that can bear repetition. I must apologise for being so long. I had a word with one of the villagers, a man I can trust. He's sending his wife up here with some woman's gear for you, you'll need a change and ... er ... other things. Ask her for anything you want. She knows some French.'

Peta thanked him tremulously, while tears started to her eyes. She was exhausted, and such unexpected consideration nearly unmanned her.

'Now don't go all feminine on me,' he warned her. 'I prefer you *au garçon*.' She blinked them back and smiled wanly. 'There is a spare room you can have,' he went on. 'No need for further doubling.' His amber eyes glinted mischievously as he recalled the various incidents of their journey. 'No wonder you were appalled when I threatened to strip and duck you!'

He laughed merrily and seated himself on the corner of the desk swinging one foot.

'I didn't find it very funny,' Peta complained. 'Nor deceiving your friend Sheikh Omar.'

'You carried it off very well, and you're not the first case of a woman posing as a man. There was that Lady Hester Stanhope who always dressed as a male and was actually buried as one. But you don't look quite the right type, not aggressive enough.'

He considered her with his head on one side.

'*Alors*, you know what everyone here will think you are?'

73

Peta *had* gone all feminine, for she blushed.

'I can guess,' she said shortly. They would believe she was Téo's woman. 'I don't do you much credit,' she added sadly, glancing down at her shabby jeans.

'Maybe you will when Meriem, that's the woman's name, has found you something to wear.' His gaze became frankly speculative.

She shook her dark head. 'Nothing would ever make me look glamorous. I'm a sports girl, you know—there I did deceive you, my name isn't Brown, it's Cartwright. You may have heard of my father, Timothy Cartwright? He's quite a celebrated writer, that's why I didn't want to involve him in this mess I'm in.'

'*Vraiment?* I've heard of him. I've read some of his books. As you know, he had been to this part of Africa, but I'm astonished that he permits his daughter to roam about on her own in such low company.'

'Keith wasn't low, and I keep telling you that nowadays we do what we like without asking our parents. I'm nearly twenty.'

'*Mon dieu*, I didn't think you could be seventeen, if that. A beardless boy. But do you mean to tell me you defied your father?'

'Not exactly. He gave up trying to control me when I left school, he knows I'm quite capable of looking after myself.'

'Your present predicament proves that you are not,' Téo pointed out, his eyes full of disapproval. 'Your father should have asserted his authority more forcibly. A good whipping might have brought you to heel. I suppose I am old-fashioned in my views, but I believe a little corporal punishment is more effective than a whole book of words.'

'What a brutal suggestion!' Peta's head went up and her nostrils flared with what Osric had termed her look of an untamed Amazon. 'Believe me, that would be no way to make me compliant.'

'Wouldn't it?' He smiled wickedly. 'Wholesome chastisement is what your unruly generation needs to teach it obedience, though I'm afraid it would come too late to chasten you.'

Her grey eyes blazed; this she had not expected. 'If you dare to lay a finger on me . . .'

He held up his hand. '*Tais-toi*, I've no intention of touching you.' Their eyes locked, his were full of laughter and hers furious indignation, and she realised he had not meant what he said. 'Thorough little spitfire, aren't you?' he told her.

'Not so very little!'

'I like tall girls, and women with spirit. More fun to subdue.'

'If you think you could subdue me . . .' she began fiercely.

'*Eh bien*, I have the whip hand, *n'est-ce pas*?' He slipped off the table and began to pace the room. 'But to be serious, what is to be done with you is a problem.' He ran his fingers through his sleek hair. 'You cannot leave the country without an exit visa, and you can't apply for that without danger of arrest.'

'Then it looks as if I'm stuck here indefinitely,' she observed with equanimity.

She did not want to leave the oasis until she had explored it, and if possible some of the surrounding country; even less did she wish to leave Téo, who intrigued her more than any man she had ever met. Even the veiled threat in his half jesting words had not scared her. It was a challenge, not an intimidation.

Presumably there must be means of communication between the Anti Atlas and Europe and if her stay was protracted she could allay her parents' anxiety, but they would not be concerned about her until they discovered she had not returned to London to attend her classes. As a last resort she might have to appeal to her father to pull strings to get her home, a thought that might occur to Téo, but she was not going to prompt him, rather she intended to encourage him in his belief that her situation was still dangerous and necessitated a long stay hidden in his oasis.

Téo did not share her satisfaction; he was looking worried. In response to her observation, he said:

'That would suit neither of us. *Enfin*, I shall, I hope, think of some way in which I can return you safely to your family.'

'Don't strain yourself,' she said flippantly, now quite at her ease. 'They won't miss me.'

'But, *ma chère jeune fille*,' he began to expostulate, when his quick ear caught the flip-flap of heelless slippers along the stone passage. 'Here comes your handmaiden.'

He went to the door, beckoning to her to follow him. A stout woman was standing on the threshold with a bundle on her head, supported by one arm. She was arrayed in the shapeless black garment similar to those worn by the Sheikh's womenfolk, with a drape over her head, though she was unveiled. Her small black eyes regarded Peta with sly curiosity. At last El Sidi had brought home a woman, but she was a girl who by native standards was supremely unattractive, such an angular lack of contours would make her a most uncomfortable bedfellow. Meriem knew her husband appreciated her own avoirdupois, but perhaps the *lallah* could be fattened up; she certainly needed dressing up!

Peta had no inkling of what was passing through the woman's mind, though she feared that, as Téo had said, she misunderstood the reason for her presence. That could not be helped, and she agreed with Meriem to the extent that Téo would have appeared to have made a poor choice. She could not compare with the girl in the photograph, she thought unhappily as she followed him down the passage with Meriem waddling in the rear, though she was at a loss as to why she continued to find the comparison so depressing. It would be most embarrassing if he became amorous, but there seemed to be little danger of that; she was obviously not his sort of woman, though he had hinted that he would like to tame her. That was of course when he had thought she might prove to be obstreperous, and his attitude towards her was still tinctured by that he had shown towards Pierre. He had not fully assimilated her metamorphosis from boy to girl.

Téo opened a door to reveal a small bedroom with whitewashed walls like the rest of the house, a narrow bed, a wooden table, chair and an old-fashioned washstand, its austerity being relieved by the bright colours of a hand-woven mat and bedspread. A square window, curtainless and guarded by a mesh framework between two shutters that could be closed at night, gave a limited view of the *palmerie*.

He said something to the woman in Mogrebi, the spoken language of the Berber people, as she dumped her load on the bed, then turned to Peta.

'Not the Crillon, but everything is clean,' he told her. 'And'—his eyes twinkled—'a little more European than your quarters last night. I've told Meriem that you would like a bath and I hope you can find something wearable among this lot.' He indicated the bundle on the bed. 'Something feminine, so I can see what my guest really looks like.'

'Nice of you to call me that,' said Peta, colouring a little, 'but if you're hoping I'll look like an odalisque I'm afraid you'll be disappointed.'

'*Nous verrons*,' he retorted, laughing. 'But now I must go. There is much I have to do. I'll join you later for a meal.'

Peta turned over the garments on the bed. There was some European underwear, which was somewhat surprising, an embroidered tunic which was long enough to serve as a dress, a towelling robe which she suspected had originated with Téo and various unidentifiable lengths of material.

Meriem returned after an interval carrying soap and towels. She also brought a man's hairbrush which she put on the table. Then in broken French she indicated that Peta should follow her, bringing the robe.

The bathroom was a narrow slit of an apartment with a zinc bath and an Elsan closet attached to the back of the house. There was no running water. This had to be carried in in jars, and Meriem, with the aid of Téo's house servant, Ismael, a dusky fellow of mixed blood whom Peta had yet to meet, had already performed this chore and steaming water rose from the bath.

'*Trop chaud?*' Meriem asked anxiously.

Peta put in a cautious finger.

'*Un peu.*'

'*Ici.*' The woman indicated a large can of cold water and withdrew.

Peta poured in some cool water, it was not actually cold, nothing was, and discarded her clothes with relief immersing herself in the bath and washing off the dust and sweat of her journey, and at the same time the last of her apprehensions. There was something about Théodore d'Argentière that inspired confidence; she was certain he would never abandon her.

Meanwhile she reflected upon the invaluable properties of water. Next to air it was the element most necessary to life, and in its secondary capacity as a cleanser never more desirable than when it was unobtainable. How she had longed for this bath throughout her hot and dusty journey! Téo was occupied in preserving water for the oasis. No man could do a nobler work, Peta thought as she splashed. She must persuade him to tell her more about it, for presumably they would spend a good many hours together.

The thought caused her a warm glow of satisfaction. What if the villagers did mistake the nature of their relationship? She did not care, and it would not harm his reputation since it was what they expected of him.

Cleansed and refreshed, she wrapped herself in the towelling robe and returned to her room where she found Meriem had removed her discarded clothes, presumably to wash them. She arrayed herself in the wide-sleeved tunic, binding it about her waist with a scarf that was also among the miscellany of drapery. She brushed her short hair, which was already nearly dry in the heat. There was no mirror in the room, so she could not see what she looked like and hoped she appeared presentable.

After folding and piling the articles Meriem had brought on a chair, she had nothing to do, and she hoped the meal Téo had mentioned would not be long delayed, for she was feeling hungry. She would have liked to go outside, but dared not do so without permission. She wondered with amusement how Téo would account for the disappearance of his cousin who had toiled with the men in the morning to be superseded by a strange young woman in the afternoon. That was his problem. It was still very hot, though the sun had started its downward journey, but it was a dry heat; if it had been humid it would have been unbearable. After staring disconsolately out of her window at the line of motionless palms with the mud-coloured buildings beyond them that showed no sign of life, she decided to return to the sitting room. There she might find something to read, and she was curious to investigate Téo's taste in literature.

There were four rooms in the house, her bedroom, Téo's room, and a dining-room opposite to the sitting-room-cum-study. As she passed the open door of the dining-room she glimpsed a table and chairs, and a turbaned individual laying a meal with ordinary cutlery, a cheering sight.

Most of the books on the home-made shelves were in

French, technical tomes dealing with engineering, drainage and minerals, but among them Peta discovered an unexpurgated edition of *The Arabian Nights* in English which she found diverting. The familiar innocent version of the tales had a very different twist in their original form!

She was curled up in one of the armchairs absorbed in the adventures of Prince Carmaralazon when Téo came in.

The rope-soled shoes he was wearing made no sound and he stood in the doorway observing her for some time before she became aware of his presence. He too had changed into white shorts and a tee-shirt, disclosing limbs burned to the colour of teak. Although not a big man, he gave an impression of whipcord energy and vitality that made larger men seem lethargic and cumbersome. Peta looked up and met the intent regard of the tawny eyes.

'Oh, it's you,' she said inadequately, surprised to find her pulse had skipped a beat. 'You don't mind me being in here?'

'Not at all. As the Spanish say, my house is yours.' He came into the room and walking to the desk began to shift through the papers. 'I was wondering if you'd be so good as to give me a hand with some of my clerical work,' he went on.

'I'd be delighted to help in any way I can, but my French grammar isn't awfully good.'

'I'll correct it. Can you type?'

'Not very well, but you don't mean to say you've got a typewriter here?'

He grinned. '*Vraiment*, I have, a portable. The blessings of civilisation are penetrating even the Anti Atlas, though as you'll have noticed, we can't rise to modern plumbing yet, nor have we any electricity, though there are tourist hotels not far away that have both. But we do have kerosene lamps and it's beginning to get dark.'

He clapped his hands and almost immediately Ismael

appeared, carrying a lamp which he set down carefully on the desk, before moving over to close the shutters over the window. He was a dignified old man with patriarchal features. Téo asked him a question to which he replied in the patois. Peta noticed he was careful to avoid looking at her.

'Our food will be ready in five minutes,' Téo told her. 'Ismael is an excellent cook—French style.' He looked at her gallantly. 'I little thought this morning that I should be sharing my dinner with a charming young lady.'

'You can cut that out,' she returned coolly. 'That's the last thing I am, and I must look a freak in this outfit. I haven't a mirror, but I've an idea it doesn't suit me.'

Téo said imperiously: 'Stand up.'

With a shrug she uncurled and rose to her feet. As she was a tall girl he only topped her by half a head, but it was enough to cause her to have to look up to him.

'You make a very attractive ... boy,' he told her, 'and perhaps it's as well I should forget you are a woman in our circumstances.'

She smiled faintly aware of a slight disappointment. 'Just as well,' she agreed, 'and that being so, you needn't stand on ceremony with me.'

His lips twitched. 'I don't intend to do that, *mademoiselle*.'

Something in his expression caused her to flush. He was not looking at her as though she were a boy, and as she turned away from him her eyes fell on the silver-framed photograph. To divert him, she asked:

'Who is that?'

He said abruptly: 'My wife.'

'Oh!' He was married, but his wife was not living with him. A dozen conjectures flashed into her mind, but she dared not question him further, for he was looking intensely forbidding, well marked brows drawn together over his high-bridged nose, his eyes like topaz stones.

'Sorry I asked,' she murmured, feeling some sort of an apology was needed.

'Why shouldn't you?' he returned indifferently.

Emboldened by this remark, she hazarded:

'She ... she's very beautiful.'

'Naturally,' he drawled. 'I wouldn't pick a plain woman.'

Whether this observation was deliberate cruelty, for Peta had never considered herself anything but plain, to pay her back for intruding upon his private life, or merely thoughtlessness, she could not decide. A gong interrupted further conversation and Téo bowed slightly:

'After you, Mademoiselle Cartwright; that is to summon us to dine.'

Ismael was standing by the door as they entered the passage and a swift exchange passed between him and his master. Then he hurried away to bring in the first course from the covered shed at the back of the house that served him for a kitchen.

The house kept fairly cool, having thick stone walls with its windows set in deep embrasures, but there was nothing ornamental or gracious about it; it could not have been planned on more functional lines. By comparison the mud-walled kasbah was picturesque.

The square deal table with a checked cloth was set with nickel cutlery and cheap glasses. The food was simple, spiced lamb and rice, tinned pineapple, cheese and biscuits followed by excellent coffee. Over it Téo began to talk about his work. He had originally come to Dar el Bali to construct the reservoir, and had stayed on to enlarge it and survey the district. He had lived most of his life in Morocco, being the child of French colonials and only leaving to be educated. The Anti Atlas region had always fascinated him, being the gateway to the wastes of the Sahara and having unlimited mineral potential. Not once did he men-

tion his wife and his marriage, and but for the photograph
Peta might have assumed she was a myth invented to frus-
trate any designs she might have upon his celibacy. As if
such an idea would ever occur to her! Yet here they were
alone together in amicable intimacy, so possibly he could be
excused if he had invented a wife, but she doubted that he
would stoop to such a ruse.

'Aren't you ever lonely?' she asked.

'Too busy,' he told her, 'and I have my trips over the
Atlas for recreation to saying nothing of'—he shot her a
wicked look—'the welcoming arms of Madame Sancé.'

'Oh yes, of course, I'd forgotten her.'

'Shocked?' he asked negligently.

'Why should I be? I'm modern.'

'*Alors*, I have my Zillah and you have your Keith—was
that his name?'

'Yes, but there wasn't anything like that between me and
Keith.'

'Like what?'

She flushed. 'Didn't you imply that your interest in
Madame Sancé was romantic, and I saw...' She stopped
confused.

'Enough to jump to conclusions,' he finished for her. 'But
appearances can be deceptive, as in your case. Let us hope
no one here jumps to them about us.'

'Does it matter if they do? Or are you afraid your
Madame Sancé would be put out if she heard ...
rumours?'

'Zillah is a *femme du monde*,' he informed her. 'She
knows men and she doesn't expect miracles.'

Peta wondered if Madame d'Argentière was another
woman of the world and treated his lapses with equal tolerance, but she had been made to realise that he did not like
references to her. The woman could expect no less if she
left her husband to live alone in the wilderness. Perhaps

that was the trouble; his wife refused to follow him to such
an outlandish place or he might consider it was too hot for
her. He had said it was no place for a woman. But he must
think a great deal of her if he could be so moved by a
chance resemblance in someone else.

The meal concluded, Téo stood up and yawned.

'*Eh bien*, I expect you're ready to go to bed,' he suggested. 'You've had a long day. Tomorrow you can tackle
my correspondence. *Bonne nuit, ma petite.*'

Which, considering her height, was not very appropriate,
but he might be referring to her mentality.

'Goodnight, *monsieur*,' she said composedly, and sought
her cell like room. A small lamp had been lighted and stood
on the table that did duty for a dresser and behind it, hanging on the wall, was a half-length mirror. Though slightly
mottled and stained, it reflected her tall slight figure in the
eastern tunic. It was not unbecoming and concealed her
lack of curves. She was deeply touched by this prompt
recognition of her needs. Ismael must have procured and
hung it while she was at dinner, and that was what Téo had
asked him to do when they encountered him in the passage.

## CHAPTER FIVE

NEXT morning Peta was awakened soon after daybreak by the arrival of Meriem, bringing in her clean shirt and jeans. The master, she indicated, was up and a bath had been prepared for the *lallah* upon his instructions. Peta knew the word meant lady, actually a lady of title, and felt she had been promoted. There was no suggestion of a swill under a bucket of well water this morning. As on the previous day she went through the bathing ritual and presented herself in the dining-room where Ismael was serving coffee, fresh bread rolls and fruit. Téo was seated at the table, but he sprang up politely as she came in, inquiring how she had slept, again a contrast to his treatment of poor Pierre.

'Like a log,' she told him as she seated herself.

He was surveying her appearance with a slight frown and she wondered of what he disapproved, for obviously there was something, but he said nothing as he resumed his chair.

'It was very kind of you to provide another bath,' she said, 'but as I know water is precious, I don't expect one every day.'

'You won't get one,' he informed her tersely, 'the reservoir is sinking fast.'

'But I'll be able to wash?'

'We'll manage enough for that.' He smiled and the atmosphere lifted. He was looking very spruce and clean himself wearing a fresh white shirt and shorts. But something seemed to be needling him, and Peta feared it might be her presence.

'There's no need to stand on ceremony with me,' she said earnestly, 'I know I must seem an imposition on your bachelor life. I can wait on myself if you show me where things are.'

'Ismael wouldn't like that,' he returned. 'He regards you as his *lallah*. We'll endeavour to put up with you.'

'That's kind of you,' she observed, 'but I hope to be useful.' She reminded him about his correspondence, and he told her he would introduce her to it when they had finished their meal.

'If you're really in earnest about it.'

'Indeed I am.'

'I do his paper work for the Caid,' he explained. 'He's officially in charge of Dar el Bali, but he finds the complexities of modern bureaucracy a little beyond him. Also there are bills and receipts to be filed, complaints to be investigated and my reports upon my findings to the Government to be compiled. If you've finished, come along.' He rose to his feet, his restless energy could never let him stay still for long. 'The stuff accumulated during my leave and I haven't yet sorted it all out.'

He opened the door for her and again as she passed him gave her a disparaging scrutiny.

Most of his business was conducted in French, which was still extensively used in commerce, but where it occurred the graceful Arabic script impressed Peta, who had often seen it used to decorate the mosques with inscriptions from the Koran.

'I wish I could read it,' she sighed.

'I have a textbook, you could start to learn it,' he suggested. 'And I could give you some lessons in the evenings.'

'Would you really?'

'Certainly, if you wish, it will be something to do.'

He seemed to genuinely want to instruct her, and Peta was elated, foreseeing the intimacy that would develop between master and pupil.

Some time later when his papers had been sorted into

neat piles, and she had undertaken to endeavour to type a formidable report on phosphate potential, she asked:

'Have I done something to displease you, *monsieur*? You keep eyeing me with disapproval.'

He looked faintly embarrassed and began to trace patterns on the desk with a paper knife shaped like a dagger.

'*Eh bien*, it's like this, Peta. As you've turned out to be a female, which makes your position here somewhat equivocal, I've told Meriem, Ismael and through them the village that you are my wife.'

Involuntarily her eyes went to Lucie's photograph.

'But ...'

'They've never seen her,' he said harshly, 'she's never come here. She ... was prevented.'

In the short tense pause that followed she waited for him to enlarge upon his statement, but he said no more. She recalled the previous morning.

'But won't they think it odd that you allowed your wife to help unload the truck?' she inquired. 'And Hassan must know I couldn't be.'

'Providentially Hassan has returned to his village,' Téo said drily. 'It seems his wife was ill. As for the others, they did not observe you closely and will accept that Monsieur Pierre has gone on to Zagora, and you arrived after dark last night. By the way, is that really your name ... Peta? It sounds so masculine.'

'Actually I was christened Perdita, but I don't like it.'

'Perdita!' he exclaimed enthusiastically. 'But that is charming, and appropriate. It means the lost one, and you have been lost, *ma chère*.'

'You can use it if you like,' she said ungraciously.

'*Alors*, but I certainly shall, and that brings me to what is wrong, Perdita, your clothes. They are not suitable for Madame d'Argentière.'

The name as applied to her seemed singularly inappropriate, nor was she sure that she wanted to pose as the mistress of his house as presumably he would expect her to do if this masquerade went through, but the more minor but pressing problem of her wearing apparel would seem to be insoluble as she hastened to point out.

'But *monsieur*, I've nothing else except that tunic thing Meriem produced,' she protested.

He considered her through narrowed lids, his eyes a glint of gold between his thick lashes.

'I've a remedy for that.'

'You are very resourceful, but why do you object so strongly to my shirt and jeans? Most girls wear them now.'

'Maybe, but in them you look like a boy, and I wish you to look like a woman. I don't want to be reminded of Pierre Brun and all the embarrassment he caused me.' Peta blushed as she recalled their shared room. 'There is a box of Lucie's things in my room, they were ... but no matter. You will find dresses in it that could be lengthened. Except for your height, you are not dissimilar in build, though she ... is more curved.'

I bet she is, Peta thought as she began to doodle with a pencil on a used envelope. She was reluctant to wear another woman's gear. Moreover, her boyish garb had always given her confidence. To appear before Téo in his wife's clothes seemed a worse usurpation than assuming his name. Also she was sure he would contrast her with his beautiful wife to her disadvantage, as he had already done when he had said she was more 'curved', and some latent feminine vanity winced at the prospect.

'Is this charade really necessary?' she asked.

'*Vraiment*.' He moved away from her and stared out of the window at the sun-baked earth. 'It seems you must reside here for some time, and I want no slur on your good name or mine. Lucie will never come here, so the charade, as you call it, will never be questioned.'

She glanced shyly at his profile which was set in stony lines. So she had been right when she had surmised that Lucie had no liking for the Moroccan desert and Téo seemed prepared to go to extreme lengths to protect herself not only physically but with regard to her good name. Impulsively she exclaimed:

'Oh, Monsieur d'Argentière, what a lot of trouble I'm causing you! You must be regretting having helped me.'

He turned towards her, saying gallantly:

'I've no regrets. It is pleasant having someone to talk to who isn't a native, and you seem to be so genuinely interested in everything, I enjoy your company. Had you been an ordinary young woman the situation would have been much more difficult, then I might have resented you. I would hate to have to maintain the semi-flirtatious attitude most women expect, but you are like the boy you pretended to be. A good companion, and as such I appreciate you.'

Peta received this assessment with mixed feelings. Apparently he could tolerate her company because it had no sexual overtones. She possessed so little feminine allure that he could forget she was a girl, accepting her as an audience when he wished to dilate upon his work and environment, and as a sop was prepared to teach her Arabic.

It was the sort of relationship she had had with Keith and fiercely sought to impose upon Osric. But Téo was very different from her student friends; he was much more mature, and she was becoming almost painfully aware of his virile masculinity. For the first time in her adult life she desired to make an emotional impact as a woman, and Téo was blandly telling her that he was relieved because she was unable to do so. She felt vaguely humiliated.

'I'd rather be regarded as a good companion than a nuisance,' she observed drily, 'But, Monsieur...'

He interrupted her by holding up his hand. '*Non*, you mustn't call me *Monsieur* as if you did not know my first name, which is Théodore. My intimates call me Téo, but I think you know that.'

'Yes, you told me, and I heard Madame Sancé use it.'

'Precisely,' he agreed urbanely, her attempt to provoke him sliding off him like oil from a seal's back, 'and if Zillah does, how much more should my wife.'

'Your pseudo-wife,' she corrected him a little bitterly.

His eyes narrowed. 'I'm not suggesting a permanent connection. You would not wish for that?'

'Of course not,' she declared hastily. 'That's the last thing I'd want.'

He raised his brows quizzically. 'We do not flatter each other, but it is best to be frank.'

But had she been frank? She had never considered marriage seriously. It was something that might or might not happen in the distant future. If she did ever marry it would probably be to a fellow athlete with a kindred interest in sport. That she should be attracted by Théodore d'Argentière was especially unfortunate. Not only was he already married, but his taste in women was for voluptuous creatures like Zillah Sancé, the antithesis of herself. Lucie appeared to be a more refined type, but then he seemed to be estranged from her.

'I made a bad husband,' he went on. 'I put my work first. Women don't like that, even if it is their bread and butter.'

'I suppose Dar.el Bali isn't everybody's ideal of a residential area,' she observed, feeling obliged to defend his absent spouse.

'*D'accord*,' he agreed, 'but it does offer a refuge.'

'Sure,' she corroborated, for it had afforded her a sanctuary. 'But, Mons ... Téo, I can't stay here indefinitely posing as your wife.'

'*Eh bien*, we must let Casablanca forget all about you, then I will seek for a way to get you out. Is it that you can't endure the place?'

'Far from it. I'm very happy to be here,' she said truthfully.

He looked gratified. '*Bon.* Then is it that you fear your parents will worry about you?' For he was sensitive enough to divine that there was something ruffling her serenity.

But that was the least of Peta's preoccupations; however, she thought he might consider she was unnatural if she said so.

'They won't for a while,' she told him. 'Later, if I'm still here, perhaps I could send them a note with your mail saying that I've decided to stay longer in Africa.'

'That could be done,' he assented, 'but surely they will be anxious to learn that you are alone out here? Or will you imply you are with this Keith, your *bien-aimé*, who perhaps they regard as your protector?'

The quizzical look that accompanied this suggestion, together with the slur upon her veracity, roused her ire, and how he did harp upon Keith, whose name she had only mentioned once or twice.

'I wouldn't lie to them,' she said indignantly, 'and I'm afraid they haven't much opinion of Keith.'

'Neither have I, for deserting you in your need.'

'He wasn't even there. There's nothing except friendship between me and Keith.' Somehow it seemed important to make him understand that. 'He's not my *bien-aimé*.'

Téo shrugged his shoulders. 'I must confess I can't distinguish between the grades of your modern relationships. You come to Morocco with a man or men and I naturally suppose one of them meant something to you.'

'Naturally you would, being a Frenchman.'

'Aren't Englishmen human also?'

'*Monsieur*—I mean Téo, you said just now you appreciated my companionship because I'm like a boy. That's how it was between Keith and me.'

'*Tiens*, you must both have water in your veins instead

of red blood,' he said with what to Peta appeared to be singular inconsistency. She returned pertly:

'And you, Téo, do you also have water in your veins?'

Their eyes met and she saw a glint in the amber depths of his that caused her heart to flutter. He laughed gaily.

'*Touché, mon enfant,* but between you and me is a gap of years. That makes a difference. Consider me as a father figure, though I am assuming the position of a husband. Now, shall we go and see what we can find to dress you for the part you are to play?'

He took a bunch of keys out of a drawer, while Peta checked a desire to point out that he was much too young to be her father. Dimly she sensed he was building up obstacles between them out of loyalty to Lucie and objections upon her part might be misunderstood.

He signed to her to follow him and led the way to his room.

This was a replica of hers except that it was a little larger and it contained a double bed. At its foot was a stout wooden chest, which when he opened the lid proved to be lined with tin as a protection against insects. He stood looking down into it with a sombre expression and Peta again felt a trespasser. According to what he had said, Lucie had never lived in that house nor occupied that double bed, but she must have meant to have come when she sent that box on in advance, and what had prevented her? Might she not eventually find the separation unbearable and make a sudden descent upon him, and if she did, would she be incensed to discover another woman had used her clothes? That Téo missed and needed her was obvious from his expression and the words he had let drop from time to time, and she, Peta, could only be a poor substitute, even though he had called her a good companion.

Téo recalled his thoughts from whatever dark labyrinth in which they were wandering and sighed.

'*Eh bien*, I will leave you now to make your selection. Take whatever will be of use to you, everything if you so desire. *Au revoir*.'

He went out so hastily she had no chance to thank him. The opening of that long-closed chest had hurt him. That it had been shut for some time was plain from the fashion of the dresses, which was of some years ago, and their deep creases; in fact one taffeta blouse had cracked where it was folded. The tissue paper was impregnated with camphor and other preservative spices. Lucie's taste was for fripperies and frills, but there were half a dozen white silk dresses in a plain loose style with deep hems that could be let down, evidently intended for morning wear. Holding one against herself, Peta realised Lucie had been plumper than herself and it would not need much alteration—those curves! There were no trouser suits, and only one pair of white slacks, but there was a good supply of filmy underwear, which though not very practical she needed badly, also diaphanous nightgowns, which she eyed a little ruefully. She would have much preferred a pair of plain pyjamas. There was as well a box of sewing tackle which would be needed.

At the very bottom of the chest she came upon a small collection of infant's clothing, romper suits, jackets and diminutive pants. Peta touched them reverently. They were evidence that there had been a child, and her intuition told her that it had died. The preservation of the small garments, the absence of any reference to it were indications of a past tragedy. That might account for Madame's disappearance; she was seeking to assuage her grief with travel and amusement, but had she no thought for the bereaved father? Téo had said the oasis was a place in which to find forgetfulness, and he solaced himself with work, but why had he chosen a spot that his wife could not tolerate, unless perhaps necessity had sent him to it. Or maybe Lucie had turned against him after the death of their child; women did sometimes become peculiar in such circumstances, but it would have been more natural if she had clung to him for comfort. Peta put back those items of this trousseau which would be of no service to her with a feeling of intense compassion for Téo, which she must never betray if she did not wish to offend him. She realised he was the type of person who hated to expose his innermost emotions to the casual onlooker, and that was all she was as yet. Only if their association ripened into real friendship could she hope to be favoured with his confidences. She wondered if he had forgotten the child's clothes were in the chest, and knew she could not mention them.

But she doubted very much if she could be content with friendship, and the pretence of being Téo's wife might become very painful to her. Though not given to self-analysis, she would have to be very stupid not to know what the attraction Téo had for her portended. She would end by falling in love with him, and even if a miracle happened and he began to see her as a desirable woman, the situation would worsen. Pride revolted from becoming another Zillah, but she could hope for no superior status while he had a wife. The unworthy thought intruded that this marriage did not seem to be very stable, Lucie might ask for her freedom or Téo demand his ... She shut the box with a slam as if to enclose in it her fantastic cogitations. It was Téo's insistence upon this attempt to regularise her position that had turned her mind in the direction of matrimony and she was not at all sure that she would want to marry him even if she could, and he certainly did not desire a legitimate union with her.

Back in her own room she proceeded to alter one of the white dresses, marvelling at the quality of the silk. Evidently the d'Argentières had not been paupers. She wondered what Meriem would make of her sudden acquisition of a wardrobe, but the Berber woman was very simple. She would regard the doings of El Sidi and his lady as the weird customs of an alien people.

The main meal in Téo's house was taken in the cool of the evening. In the intense heat of midday everyone dozed and Téo often skipped lunch altogether as he had done on the day of her arrival. He had instructed Ismael to provide Peta with refreshment whenever she asked for it, but when it was so hot, all she required was a drink. She worked all that afternoon on her dress, a slow task, for she was a poor seamstress. Téo was out visiting the kasbah; he spent a good many hours with the Caid. As the furnace heat began to subside, she arrayed herself in her creation. The soft silk draped her angular limbs and the colour was flattering to her sunburnt complexion. She brushed her hair hard to restore some of its gloss which the heat tended to make dry and brittle. Meriem had produced for her use several pairs of native babouches which Téo had bought from her. The villagers made them themselves. As the slippers were the feminine variety they had embroidered toecaps, but they hardly gave a chic finish to her ensemble.

The mottled mirror showed her a not unpleasing image and she made a face at her reflection.

'Let us hope my lord and master will be satisfied,' she said to it. 'After all that labour and pricked thumbs!'

He was more, he was obviously startled, but whether it was because she appeared so different from Lucie in her dress or because of her metamorphosis into a girl, she was not quite sure.

'Is that feminine enough for you?' she asked, revolving before him, very conscious of the intent assessment in his eyes.

'*Charmante*,' he told her. 'Such beautiful legs you have, why do you conceal them in those horrible trousers?'

Peta looked down at her slim brown shins and shapely

ankles, innocent of stockings. Her skirt ended below her knees.

'Poor legs, they'll be horribly vulnerable ... to insect bites and scratches,' she said, laughing, knowing they were also vulnerable to masculine appraisal. Then because something in his eyes faintly embarrassed her, she told him:

'I'm so unused to skirts I can't walk in them gracefully.'

'You would always be graceful whatever you wore,' he returned.

'Thank you, kind sir. That must be because I've been taught co-ordination.'

'Do you always have to be so clinical?' he asked with faint irritation. 'Why not accept you were born with natural grace? But let it be,' as he saw she was about to contest that statement. 'I've brought you the necessary trimmings.'

He was extracting a small box from his pocket.

'Trimmings?'

A wicked sparkle came into his eyes. 'Naturally you will have to wear a ring, and while I was about it, I procured a necklace from the same source. You know the Moroccans are expert at silverware. The Caid's wife had ordered a selection on approval from Marrakech, and I took the opportunity of obtaining the necessary.'

He opened the box and drew out a necklace of exquisitely wrought silver, such as was moulded in the souks of the big towns, and a silver ring.

'But do the shops send things out here?' Peta asked, surprised.

'The old merchant brought them himself, he wouldn't miss the chance to do some bargaining. Hold out your hand.'

Somewhat reluctantly she held out her left hand, for to wear his ring which should be a solemn pledge seemed almost sacrilegious when it was to support a lie. He shook his head.

'The right one, please, for a marriage ring. I am French.'

'The left one is supposed to be nearer to the heart.'

'Mere foolish sentiment.'

'And you are not sentimental?' she inquired, thinking of the cherished baby clothes, or perhaps he did not know they were there.

'Not in the least. Your right hand, please.'

He took her slim brown hand in his and dexterously pushed on the ring.

'It fits,' he observed with satisfaction, retaining her hand. He turned it over, looking at the palm, noting the distance between her thumb and the rest of her hand. 'An artistic hand, a generous hand, yet you give all to *le sport*.'

Peta laughed self-consciously.

'I didn't know you were a palmist!'

'I see what is obvious, and I've many hidden talents.'

'I'm sure you have.' She looked at his fingers holding hers, browner than hers, long and muscular. Strong shapely hands, capable of guiding his destiny—and hers.

'As regards sport,' she went on, aware of a slight tension between them, 'I've yet to find a more worthwhile object on which to bestow my energies.'

'But you will,' he said absently, stroking her fingers. 'You are still very young. I hope he will be worthy of you when you find him.'

'Must that always be the supreme goal of a woman's life—a man?' she asked scornfully, jerking away her hand.

'Of course, if she is to be happy.'

Peta turned away her head. With a flash of clairvoyance she knew she could be happy without any of her former interests if she could spend her future with Téo. Pipe dreams, she thought, mentally shaking herself; she had been caught by an attractive exterior, the magnetism of his male vitality, but she did not really know him nor what made him tick. He was no less fascinating because he was still an enigma to her.

He picked up the necklace and held it out to her. 'Put this on,' he bade her.

'I ... I don't think that's necessary,' she said ungraciously.

'But I do. *Madame ma femme* must be suitably adorned.' Then as she still hesitated, he added irritably: 'Do you imagine such a present is a prelude to seduction? If such was my intention I'd offer more than that.'

Uncharacteristically she flushed vividly. 'Of course not, but you've done enough for me without giving me trinkets.'

'*C'est rien*, a trifling piece of silverware to be a souvenir of your stay in Morocco.'

Instantly her reluctance seemed absurd. Meekly she took the necklace and laid it on her neck, the metal felt cool and heavy like a fetter.

'Let me fasten it for you,' Téo suggested, stepping behind her.

She felt his fingers against her nape as he secured the clasp and a tremor ran down her spine. Never before had she been so affected by a man's touch; it was the prelude to a whole new field of experience and emotion opening before her, but unfortunately she must not explore it, for not only was Téo not free, but he was also indifferent to her. Was he really so, or was it assumed because of their unconventional situation? She glanced at him sideways under her lashes, which were long and dark, a provocative look, but wholly innocent. She had no conscious desire to seduce him.

Téo moved away from her with a triumphant laugh.

'Already you become more feminine under the influence of skirts and jewellery.'

'But I thought you didn't want me to be feminine,' she objected.

He looked at her sensuously. 'That was my good sense speaking, and *hélas*, we must let it rule us if we don't wish for complications.'

Greatly daring, excited by the gleam in his eyes, she said archly: 'A few such complications might enliven life in the desert.'

He smiled wryly.

'Do not try to tempt me, *ma chère*, you are innocent, *n'est-ce pas*? I should hate myself if you left me the worse for knowing me.'

She turned her back upon him and walked away to the window, biting her lips with vexation. What demon had got into her to make a remark that had laid her open to such a repulse? He thought she was naïve and green, unlike Zillah with whom he would have had no scruples, though neither were in love. Love? What had put that idea into her head? Could a girl fall in love with a man she had known only a few days, and another woman's man at that? Not that she need have any qualms about Lucie—if she expected fidelity, she should look after her husband, but compared with the woman in the photograph Peta was sure Téo would regard her as a poor substitute for his wife's loveliness. Worse and worse, what did she want? Téo to make love to her? Certainly not, and yet ... and yet ...

The dinner gong put an end to her musings and they went into the other room to eat. Over the meal Téo became impersonal, talking about the country and its customs. He told her of the Blue People, the Tuaregs from the Western Desert, who still rode camels and came in to the oases to collect basic supplies every so often, a people who regarded the North as a horrible place full of motor cars, houses, pavements, railways and other harassments, though they had never seen it and probably never would. Of the Berber girls who danced at festivals and still tattooed their faces. Peta listened with her eyes on her plate, thus missing the appreciative glances he threw her from time to time. With her Egyptian profile, dense black hair, her slender neck rising from the silver necklet that might have been a small pectoral, and her clinging white dress, she presented an unusual and arresting appearance, and when she finally raised her eyes to his face their clear grey was unexpected.

Téo broke off his discourse to say: 'Nerfertiti until you look at me, and then...' He spread his hands in a Gallic gesture. 'Has anyone ever told you your eyes are like mountain tarns on a grey day reflecting the shrouded sky?'

'Is that a compliment?' she asked. 'It sounds gloomy.'

'Ah no! Not gloomy, beautiful, to one who has lived long in this sun-shrivelled land. The soft grey of rain washed sky and water becomes an exquisite memory. Peace and serenity are surely expressed by grey.'

'Then my eyes belie me for I'm not a serene person,' Peta told him. 'I'm restless and adventurous.' But she was pleased by his comments.

'That's because you haven't found your anchor,' he began, and she hastened to intervene to forestall another discourse upon marriage and domesticity being a woman's destiny.

'I don't need one. I keep telling you, I'm a sportswoman. The stadium, swimming pool and tennis court are my right environment. My ambition is to become an Olympic champion.'

But why did such a future no longer seem paramount?

'*Tiens*, what energy!' Téo exclaimed with mock horror. 'Truly you are an Amazon, though not——' His eyes fell to the slight curve of her breasts revealed by the clinging silk, '...multilated as they were. I suppose you're also expert in the art of self-defence?'

'Of course.' But he was not Osric; she had no wish to use her art against him.

He grinned impishly. 'I must be careful not to provoke you.'

'I'm sure you never would,' she retorted, her eyes on her

plate again. Téo considered her for a long moment with a quizzical expression.

'You are a surprising young woman,' he observed at length. 'But what happens when you grow older, *ma fille*? An athlete's career is a short one and middle age is very long.'

'Oh, I suppose I'll rest on my laurels,' she said flippantly. At twenty the middle years seem very remote. 'Or perhaps I'll marry and have children.'

The animation died out of his face and it became still as stone.

'Hostages to fortune,' he declared. Peta recalled the baby's clothes, pathetic mementoes of loss, and wished she had guarded her tongue.

After a pause he went on more brightly: '*Alors*, since you are so tough (she winced inwardly at his description; tough was an unglamorous word and she did not wish to appear so to him), perhaps you would like to come out with me tomorrow? I'm going up one of the river gorges. It'll be hot, dusty and rough going, so I warn you.'

'I'd love to come,' she cried eagerly, her face flashing into vivid animation. 'I don't care how rough it is. Do we travel in the truck?'

'No, I've an old army jeep, not very elegant, but most of this terrain is too much for a car. I would prefer——' he looked at her sternly, 'that you wear a dress.'

'But jeans would be much more suitable for such an expedition,' she protested.

'Not for Madame d'Argentière.'

'But the tourists . . .'

'My wife is not a tourist.'

'Oh, very well.'

She thought his prejudices were absurd, but for some reason, possibly because it reminded him of the intimacy they had shared on their journey, he disliked seeing her in

101

her boyish garb. He was very anxious to obliterate the image of Pierre Brun, but he was showing scant regard to her physical comfort.

'Are you sure you wouldn't prefer me to appear in a haik and veil?' she asked pertly. 'That might flatter the tyrannical streak in you.'

'I've no wish to appear a tyrant,' he returned, 'but I insist upon being master in my own house.' He smiled mischievously and his eyes gleamed golden. 'I know how to keep little girls in order even if they are tough.'

'Oh, do you!' They had finished their coffee and Peta stood up, looking down at him with disdain. 'You sound very confident.'

'I am.' He grinned at her. 'And not such a little girl either.' He sprang up and came to her, putting his hands upon her shoulders. '*Eh bien*, my young Amazon, could you throw me in a wrestling bout?'

Her eyes widened in astonishment at such a question which was at such variance with his previous insistence upon her assumption of wifely dignity.

'What a ludicrous suggestion,' she exclaimed uncertainly. 'I ... I think my technique would be useless against you.'

'Now I wonder why.' His brown face crinkled with laughter. 'Can it be you're learning to submit to masculine superiority?'

His hands moved over her shoulders, seeking the muscles beneath her smooth skin and closed over her biceps. 'Not developed enough to be disfiguring.'

'You think I'm some sort of freak, don't you?' she flung at him bitterly.

'*Tiens*, not at all.' He dropped his hands. 'You have merely developed your body at the expense of your emotions. You're completely unawakened.' He sighed. 'Some man will have great pleasure in bringing you to life.'

The question nearly escaped her, 'Why not you?' but she

bit it back. Though his words were provocative he did not mean them personally, and he was wrong, her senses were more than half awake. Something must have shown in her eyes, for abruptly he moved away from her and said coldly:

'As we'll be making a very early start you'd better go to bed, *mon enfant*. Goodnight.'

'Goodnight, Téo,' she returned, but she lingered. 'I hope you sleep well.'

'Reciprocated.' He swung round and his eyes were glittering. 'Go to bed,' he bade her harshly.

Peta went. He had called her a child and as such he wished to regard her, but she was not a child and he was well aware of it, and after all, Lucie d'Argentière was very far away.

# CHAPTER SIX

PETA rose at the first pale glimmerings of dawn aroused by the sound of a motor vehicle outside. Looking through her window, she saw the jeep, a squat dark shape against the brightening sky, parked beside the house, and Ismael wrapped in a hooded d'jellaba to protect him from the morning chill carrying a case of provisions to stow in its interior. It was blessedly cool before the sun came up to scorch the land with its blistering rays. Though there was never much rain in that country Peta had been told the climate could be quite pleasant in autumn and winter, but it was still only September, when the sun retained the torrid heat of a desert summer.

After a hurried toilet she went to join Téo over a quick breakfast, carrying her d'jellaba, which she laid over the back of a chair. Noticing his frown, she said quickly:

'I'll wait to put it on in the jeep, but I must have some protection from the sun and dust.'

'Wear it by all means, but not here. My men might recognise it.'

She blushed as she remembered how she had clung to it to conceal her figure and he went on with a merry twinkle in his eye. 'Though even they couldn't mistake you for a boy now. You've changed, *ma femme*, in the last two days. There's a bloom on you now that is unmistakably female, you couldn't deceive the least observant eyes.'

The change was his doing; under his influence she was emerging like a butterfly from its chrysalis from the sheath of adolescence that had enclosed her emotional development so long. She hoped he did not suspect that—and it

104

seemed a little unnecessary to address her as his wife when they were alone.

She was beginning to understand that Téo possessed a sardonic sense of humour which her position seemed to tickle. She knew that if she protested he would retaliate with some audacious riposte with the intention of embarrassing her. He did not mean to be unkind, but he could not resist teasing her, so she let his remarks pass without comment.

Téo was wearing a light wool sweater and his Arab headcloth, a combination that was slightly incongruous, but many of the Moors now wore a mixture of Eastern and Western apparel.

Peta slipped out to the jeep while Téo was giving some last moment instructions to Ismael, and was sitting in the seat next the driver wrapped in her gown when he came to join her. He was carrying a large native hat such as the women of the Rif wore and a pair of sunglasses.

'More protective clothing for you,' he told her. She was touched by his thoughtfulness, and put the hat upon her head. The glasses, which were a spare pair of his, she reserved for later on. She knew they would be most unbecoming, but she did not think the hat was much more so.

He seemed in excellent spirits and was whistling gaily as they drove through the village. She recognised the tune as a love song.

'I thought the Indian Love Lyrics were outdated,' she remarked.

'But you recognised it, so they can't be completely dead,' he pointed out, and began to sing in a rich baritone:

'Less than the dust beneath thy chariot wheels.'

'That's a woman's song,' she objected.

'But very appropriate. There is, as you perceive, plenty of dust beneath the wheels of my jeep, and the desert

105

women are supposed to be subservient.'

'I'm glad you say supposed to be, for I don't believe they are.'

'Of course they're not. They run the home and often their man as well, and as they have the right to vote now, they may end by running the country. But the song refers to the state of the lady's affections. To the object of them she was less than the dust, the weed beside his door and the rust that never stained his sword, so she preferred suicide to his neglect. All very touching and quite unrealistic. A sensible woman would transfer her love to a more appreciative recipient.'

'You're a cynic, but I fancy the lady in the song hadn't any choice, she was probably a member of his harem whom he had overlooked. Do you regret the passing of the seraglios, Téo? They must have made a man feel very superior.'

'Who wants to feel superior?' he returned unexpectedly. 'A man's wife should be his equal and his mate.'

'Is yours?' The question slipped out without pause for thought. She was immensely curious about his relationship with his wife.

He glanced at her blankly and made no reply, accelerating so violently that the jeep gave a jolt that nearly threw her out of her seat. Dust rose in a cloud from under its wheels and it swayed from side to side of the narrow track.

'Oh, don't,' she gasped, coughing, then added meekly, 'I'm sorry.'

He said nothing, but he slackened speed. Presently he began to point out objects of interest, but there was no more singing. Peta was furious with herself for quenching his gaiety with her unfortunate question. She should know by now that the absent Lucie was taboo as a subject of conversation and she had blundered. But why was Téo so cagey about her? What was wrong?

They crossed an area of sand dunes and then the mountains came to meet them, vast stony piles of rock. The road wriggled through a cleft in this formidable wall, which eventually widened into a fertile valley through which ran a river. The level spaces along its banks were cultivated with fodder crops, and where the ground started to rise were fruit trees, orange, lemon, almond and olives. Above them again were date palms before the barren waterless regions of stony hillsides that enclosed the oasis.

Téo came to a halt in the shadow of a sheer cliff.

'I want to take a look at the rock fall over there.' He indicated a gash in the hillside. 'There was a landslide there some weeks back and some interesting features were revealed. Will you stay in the jeep, it's too hot and rough walking for you, or would you like to go for a stroll?'

'I'd like to have a look round,' said Peta. 'I suppose the natives are friendly?'

'They won't molest you and they're too proud to beg,' he assured her. 'Don't go too far, I shan't be long.'

'Only to that kasbah.' She pointed to a crumbling mud building on a spur reaching out into the river. 'Does anybody live there?'

'No, it's a ruin. Take care not to sprain your ankle. *Au revoir.*'

They parted to go off in different directions. Peta sauntered along the road beside the river, a somewhat bizarre figure in d'jellaba and big hat. There were the usual mud brick slit-windowed houses enclosed by high walls, a few black-robed figures were working in the fields, goats and hobbled donkeys browsed by the road side. She was enchanted to come upon what looked like a field of roses still in bloom, from which she knew rosewater, much favoured in that country, was distilled. She lingered awhile absorbing their fragrance, thinking of the Persian poet who sang of roses and nightingales and wine. She wondered if there were any nightingales in that vicinity. Finally she essayed the short climb up to the kasbah.

It was, as Téo had said, a ruin, most of the roofs having fallen in from the buildings surrounding its various courts. There were fragments of mosaic and broken tiles lying about showing that it had once been a fine place, but Peta had read enough Moroccan history to know that less than a century ago these castles had been the strongholds of fierce tribes carrying on not only feuds with other tribes, but families against families and brother against brother, and these ruined walls must have witnessed many a scene of horror.

Reflecting on the bloodthirsty past, she stepped out into what had been the main courtyard where a few wilted almond trees still struggled to survive. The once massive doors had gone and part of the crenellated wall was down, giving a view of the cultivations below her bathed in harsh sunlight interspersed with violet shadows, the last greenness of crops and trees wilting in the late summer heat. She wondered how long Téo would be, for she was thirsty, though not very hungry, and then she froze. What had looked like a dead branch on a pile of rubble had moved.

Peta had a horror of snakes; it was a physical allergy, nothing to do with normal fear, as some people experience in the presence of cats. Her body broke out into a clammy sweat and she stood petrified, unable to move as the brown sinuous body slithered over the stones. Then she saw Téo coming through the ruined gateway, but was too paralysed to call a warning to him.

The snake decided the locale was becoming too populated for comfort, and with the speed of a whiplash disappeared into a hole, like the passing of an evil dream.

Peta leaned against the mud wall behind her, trembling in every limb.

'*Mon dieu*, but what has happened?' Téo cried, running towards her.

She raised terrified eyes to his; her hat had fallen off and she was bareheaded.

'I saw a snake.'

'A snake?' He looked about him. 'Where is it?'

'It ... it's gone, but ... but ...'

And then she was in his arms, clinging to him, trembling violently, her head beneath his chin.

'You're not hurt?' he asked her anxiously. 'It didn't bite you?'

'No, oh, no! I can't bear the things.' Her voice was a thin thread.

Téo held her close against him and gradually the shuddering left her limbs. She became aware of who was holding her, of the gentle pressure of his arms, the soothing words he was whispering in her ears. He was comforting her as if she were a frightened child, but she was not a child and he ought not to be holding her. She tried to free herself, but ineffectually, for he did not release her.

'I ... I'm a fool,' she said tremulously, 'but honestly, the sight of those things makes me feel physically ill.'

'So my Amazon has a vulnerable spot,' he said softly, tightening his clasp, the arm across her back pressing her body against his. The other was across her shoulders, and with his hand he raised her chin. 'Perhaps this will make you feel better.'

His mouth hard upon hers did not exactly do that, but it did give her a new sensation, driving out all recollection of the snake. Involuntarily her arms went round his neck. His grip of her became cruelly constricting, and his kisses longer and more demanding. Peta lost all sense of time and place as she responded to the wave of passion that engulfed them. She had never dreamed nor even imagined that she was capable of the sensual desire that overwhelmed her. Not that she was conscious of thought, she only knew she wanted Téo to hold her and go on kissing her for ever.

It was he who recovered first, thrusting her away from him so violently that she nearly fell. Covertly she watched him from under her lashes, noticing he had gone pale under his tan, as he took out his handkerchief and mopped his brow. She was not offended by his action, she knew he had been as deeply stirred as she had been, and exultation flooded her being and shone in her eyes. Téo was not indifferent to her; he was as drawn to her as she was to him. She had shown him she was neither a child nor a boy but a woman capable of responding to his adult needs. She had forgotten Lucie and the barrier between them. Here in the deep south the sun ripened all things early, and her cool, almost sexless immaturity had burst its bonds and come to throbbing life.

'*Tiens!*' Téo exclaimed. 'I had no idea you had so much fire in you.'

She smiled happily. 'It is you who have ignited it.'

But there was no answering warmth in his face. Instead he said ruefully:

'This should never have happened. Truly the snake has entered Eden.'

Even the reminder of the sinuous cause of her panic could not damp her rapture, though she threw an involuntary glance towards its hole.

'It had to happen,' she cried vehemently. 'Téo, it's Kismet, it's fated. Our meeting at Chaouen, your presence at Casa when I needed you. You brought me here and now ...' She took a step towards him her eyes shining, but to her dismay he retreated.

'Come down to earth, *mon enfant*,' he said gently, 'and be your age. You're too old for fairy tales. I'm no romantic desert sheikh, nor do I believe in fate. I'm a hardboiled, disillusioned man, and I apologise for my lack of manners. This primitive land encourages primitive urges, and I've been denied female company too long.'

110

Peta stared at him in bewilderment. 'Was that all it was?' she faltered. 'I just happened to be handy when you ... Oh, no, Téo, it's more than that. Say it was more than that!'

He could not meet the reproach in her eyes, but he did not soften.

'Come, Perdita, surely you're not ignorant of male reactions?' he asked her. 'You who've travelled alone with youths? Shall we go back to the jeep? I could use a drink and I'm sure you could do with one.'

She wondered dully if he were being deliberately cruel or whether he felt he must snub her because of Lucie, his wife. But she had not stood in his way when he was with Zillah. Slowly the realisation came to her that what for her had been a unique experience was to him only the automatic response to a woman in his arms, and he was regretting his lack of control and apologising for it. She longed to be able to recall her impulsive and silly speech about fate linking them together. How naïve and absurd it must have sounded to him, as his subsequent remarks had indicated. She had seen a mirage of water where there was only arid desolation. Then she recalled his stricture upon flirtatious girls and his dislike of having to play up to them; would he now believe she was one of them?

She drew herself up proudly, searching for words to hurt him to cover her own wound.

'I've been talking a load of rubbish,' she said disdainfully. 'You upset me—I didn't realise you were that sort of man. It will make this pretence you've insisted upon impossible if you can't control yourself.'

'May I point out that you hurled yourself into my arms?' he reminded her suavely.

'And you took that as an invitation when actually I was terrified?' she accused him.

He shrugged his shoulders. 'Suppose we forget it? It's

not important. Didn't you tell me you were an emancipated modern girl?'

'Oh, I am,' she concurred. Some perverse imp of reck-lessness caused her to add: 'But modern girls don't stop at kissing.'

'But I'm an old-fashioned man, and I do.'

'You surprise me. What about Madame Sancé?'

'That's different.' Then he flashed at her irritably, '*Mon dieu*, girl, do you want to be seduced?'

'Of course not.' She was shaken back into sanity by his blunt question. 'I'm sorry, it's the heat and the snake, I ... I'm not quite myself.' She turned away and whispered, 'I only want to be loved.'

She had not meant him to hear, but he did, and his face softened.

'Ah, *mon enfant*, love is a wholly different matter and has nothing to do with what happened just now. Come along.' He retrieved her hat and jammed it on her head. 'It's getting unpleasantly hot here. I shouldn't wonder if you hadn't got a touch of the sun without a head covering.'

'That's it,' she clutched at the straw he offered to save her dignity. 'My head's going round and round. Let's get back to the jeep.'

She hurriedly started the descent from the kasbah and he called after her:

'*Prends garde!* Do you want to break your neck?'

Resisting an impulse to say she did not care if she did, Peta allowed him to overtake her. After a slight hesitation, he offered her his arm, which she refused with a short:

'I can manage, thank you.' She had noted the hesitation.

Over their picnic lunch she laughed and chattered with an attempt at normality that was a little overdone. Since Téo wanted to wipe out the whole unfortunate incident she would do her best to abet him, but though he might forget it, she never could. Téo had become the centre of her universe, but to him she was less than the dust.

That evening he started her lessons in Arabic, sitting at some distance from her, and was so cool and impersonal that the episode of the morning might never have occurred. She began to doubt its reality herself; had it been some desert phantasm that had temporarily deranged her? It seemed impossible that the cold self-contained man sitting opposite to her could have kissed her so passionately.

When he closed the book, he told her:

'I'm expecting a visit from the Minister in charge of this province the day after tomorrow. He will be flying here from Ouarzazate by helicopter and will be here for *déjeuner*. He'll expect a French meal.'

'But I thought the Caid . . .?'

'He's only the village headman, this other is much more important. You'll need to be on your best behaviour.'

'Surely I needn't see him?'

'*Cela va sans dire.*' He grinned. 'Were we natives he would not expect you to appear, but we are French and civilised, you understand. Ismael will know what to cook, but you must receive him as his hostess.' He surveyed her white dress critically. 'Wasn't there anything more chic in that box for you to wear?'

'There were some very smart dresses, but they'd need a lot of altering, and I'm no dressmaker.'

'Get Meriem to help you.'

'But won't she think it . . . odd?'

'She believes you lost your luggage en route, but it does not matter what she thinks. You will see to it?'

'I'd much rather stay in my room,' she persisted.

It was one thing to wear a ring and pretend to be who she was not to preserve their reputations with the servants, quite another to entertain an important personage posing as Madame d'Argentière. Surely Téo must see that, but he remained unsympathetic.

'He will have been told I've a woman living with me,' he pointed out, 'and how can I explain you except as my wife? Oh, he's never met Lucie, if that's what's bothering you.'

'I'll be in a false position,' she murmured, the quick colour staining her face.

'You've been that ever since you left Casa, and Madame d'Argentière is a more suitable role for you than Pierre Brun.'

'Couldn't you say I was ill?'

'You can't stew all day in that box of a room of yours. You will do as I request, please, Perdita.'

Her eyelids flickered. 'Is that an order?'

'Definitely.'

She sighed. 'What a tyrant you are!'

'I'm considering your comfort.'

Physically perhaps, but mentally not at all. The fiction she was being asked to preserve was all the more trying because she wished it were true, but she knew she would have to do what he commanded.

'I hear and obey,' she acquiesed, making a mock salaam.

'*Bon,* that's what I like to see, wifely subservience,' he told her with a mischievous glint in his eyes.

'So Madame d'Argentière is a doormat?' she asked provocatively.

He winced. 'Please to keep your tongue off her,' he said sharply.

She had again trespassed on forbidden ground and been duly snubbed. The marriage, she felt sure, could not be a happy one.

Peta spent the next day altering a striped silk dress, Meriem proving to be skilful with her needle, which was perhaps hardly surprising as the Berber women made their own clothes and were clever at embroidery. Ismael was polishing everything that could be polished and the ugly little house was filled with an air of expectancy. The coming guest was not only a V.I.P., but he held the future of the province in his hands.

The arrival of the helicopter aroused great excitement among the villagers, especially the children, who swarmed out to welcome it, at risk of their lives. Peta waited in the house in some trepidation, fearing to make some blunder. Ismael was preparing a meal of curry and rice to be followed by sweet omelettes, fruit, cheese and coffee. The fruit had been brought in that morning, ripe figs, oranges and dates.

The striped silk was multi-coloured with a little short-sleeved crimson jacket also of silk. It had a crossover bodice with a deep V neck, thereby displaying Téo's necklet to advantage. Although she did not realise it the bright colours enhanced Peta's sunburned complexion and night-dark hair. Téo gave her a cursory inspection and pronounced himself satisfied; there was a gleam in his tawny eyes as he regarded her which might have been either derision or admiration.

The minister was a short stout person wearing a well cut European suit. Peta thought how much more distinguished Téo looked beside him in a formal suit of white drill, so lean and elegant compared with the other's rotundity.

The visitor shook hands with her and paid her several compliments in reply to the carefully prepared words of greeting Téo had taught her. Privately he thought she was much too thin to be appetising. Most of the conversation throughout the simple meal was between him and his host about the results of Téo's prospecting.

While he talked, Téo's eyes frequently rested upon her, and she thought despondently he was contrasting her unfavourably with his wife's appearance in the borrowed dress and found her gauche. She was unaware that her sports training had given her a grace of movement that was apparent whatever she wore and her long limbs were

115

shapely; well shaped also was her head upon her long throat, rising from well moulded shoulders, while the bone structure of her face had the comeliness that outlasts mere prettiness.

Over coffee the guest turned to her and congratulated her upon her courage.

'Thank you,' she returned, eyes demurely cast down, 'but in what way am I brave?'

'To accompany your husband into the desert and stay with him through the hottest part of the year. Not many Western women are so dutiful.'

'It's love,' Téo declared with a wicked glint in his eyes. 'She cannot bear to be parted from me.'

'*Charmant*,' the visitor murmured, his Eastern reticence faintly offended by this intimate disclosure, while Peta blushed fierily. Téo need not have said that.

The Minister took his leave soon after the meal after presenting Peta with a box of sweets, which she noticed with amusement were American candies, and Téo accompanied him to visit the Caid.

The noise of the helicopter's engines announced his departure towards evening. Peta was languidly studying her Arabian grammar, oppressed by the ambiguity of her position. She had acted hostess in another woman's house, wearing her clothes and appropriating her husband. If Lucie ever got to hear about it she would never forgive Téo.

He returned as soon as the helicopter had taken flight. He stood in the doorway regarding Peta so intently that she wondered what she had done to annoy him.

'I hope I didn't disgrace you,' she said nervously.

'On the contrary, you behaved admirably. A perfect representation of a modest, dutiful wife, as his high and mightiness indicated.'

'You needn't have put in that bit about love,' she told him indignantly. 'You embarrassed the poor man.'

Téo laughed. 'I was explaining your hardihood in accompanying me to such a barbarous outpost. Only love
could persuade a woman to accept such surroundings, and
not always then.'

A note of bitterness crept into his voice, emboldening
Peta to ask: 'They were too much for Madame d'Argentière?'

'You couldn't expect a Parisienne to stomach them.'

Peta looked down at her silken skirts, the cut of which
she feared she and Meriem had spoiled by their alterations.
So Lucie d'Argentière came from Paris, and perhaps she
had gone back there. While she debated whether she dared
question further, Téo said abruptly:

'*Eh bien*, we do not seem to progress with solving your
problem, and we may have to do so very soon. Our august
visitor was disappointed by my findings and though he was
impressed by the fertility of the oasis, due to the reservoir,
he considers further development uneconomical.'

'Does that mean you'll be leaving?' she asked, dismayed.

He sat down on the arm of the chair opposite to her,
staring at his feet.

'I invested my own money in the reservoir. I wanted to
show them what could be done to make the desert bloom,
but *hélas*, Morocco is a poor country, it cannot afford such
experiments.'

'But if the results are so good?'

'The returns are too slow and too local. The Berbers of
the Anti Atlas have always had it tough, their needs aren't
given priority in Rabat.'

He fell into a brooding silence which Peta hesitated to
break. She looked round the plain little room which already
seemed like home to her, but only because it was Téo's.
The austere life between the mountains and the desert was
very different from that depicted in romances. Here were no
sumptuous tents, no oriental luxuries, no prancing horses,

only poverty-stricken villagers in mud huts, this stone box and a battered jeep. Nor was Téo a glamorous sheikh in flowing robes, but a work-worn man usually clad in shorts and shirt, who at that moment was facing defeat for lack of government backing.

She said at length: 'At least you've done something to help Dar el Bali.'

'I've made a duckpond where I dreamed to create a lake,' he said gloomily, 'and they'll let it silt up when I've gone.' He looked at her with a faint smile. 'When you're back in the swinging city will you sometimes think of the bleak hills of the Anti Atlas and the lone toiler at their foot, or will you dismiss it all as an unpleasant dream best forgotten?'

'It's not unpleasant,' she declared violently. 'I'll never forget this place ... nor you.'

Their eyes met in a long searching gaze until Peta turned her head away, stifling the sob that rose in her throat.

'So the desert has laid its spell on you too,' he said softly. 'You must leave before the wrench becomes too great.'

'But where am I to go?' she asked miserably, for surely he must know he was the wizard who weaved the desert magic. 'And how can I go?'

'I think I can arrange that, with your concurrence,' he told her, 'but the plan needs a little more thought before I expound.' He studied her with an enigmatical expression, then sighed. '*Eh bien*, I must go back to the Caid. I'll not be in to dinner, but Ismael will serve yours. As I'll not be back until late, I'll say goodnight.'

'Goodnight,' she responded dully.

She listened to the sound of his footsteps along the passage and heard the slam of the door.

It was the man who had laid his spell upon her, not the desert, and the wrench would be very great.

# CHAPTER SEVEN

Two mornings later Peta came out of her room to find Téo wrestling with the telephone. This was a modern amenity that did exist in the oasis, but the connection was very poor. Téo was muttering oaths in three languages. He jammed the receiver down when he saw her and followed her into the dining-room, where Ismael had just set down the steaming coffee pot.

'It is ended,' he said dramatically as he took his seat.

Peta lifted scared eyes to his. 'What has?'

'My life here. As soon as I can wind up my affairs I must leave for France.'

Peta was glad to find her hand was steady as she poured out the coffee; she felt suddenly weak with a constricted sensation about her heart. Though Téo had mentioned that his work might be finishing he had said nothing definite about leaving. She wondered if he had been dismissed over the telephone.

'It's ... it's very sudden,' she murmured.

'Yes.' She noticed he had an air of suppressed excitement. 'My grandfather has died and I find myself the heir to an estate in France, a *mas*—that is a sort of farm—in the Camargue. I am, you see, the last of my family.'

'But ... but I thought you were born in Morocco.'

'I was, but I'm still French. My parents came here, but the remainder of the family stayed in France.' His eyes gleamed like topazes. 'I never thought the old man would bequeath it to me. Congratulate me.'

'I do, or shouldn't I offer my condolences? You were fond of your grandfather?'

'No, he was a surly old miser,' Téo told her cheerfully. 'I tried to borrow from him once for my project here, but he wouldn't part with a centime, and now it's all mine.' He looked younger and brighter, wholly different from the tired, defeated man after the Minister's visit. Peta tried to rejoice with him, but her heart felt like lead.

'I'll have to go home,' Téo went on. 'No inducement to remain here, because the only stipulation made apparently is that I shall not waste his wealth upon the ungrateful revolutionaries in Africa, so the solicitor tells me. He could never reconcile himself to Morocco's independence.'

'But ... but won't you be sorry to go?' she asked as she handed him a second cup of coffee.

'No, I've outworn my usefulness here, as our friend the Minister hinted. I can do more worth while work on my grandfather's estate.'

'And when do you go?' She was wondering desperately what was to become of her. Surely he could not intend to walk out and leave her to shift for herself? Yet with this exciting prospect opening before him, how could she expect him to consider her, who had always been a nuisance to him?

'Not for a few weeks.' Téo drained his coffee. 'There are several things to be settled first. Primarily the question of your passport.'

'You know I can't apply for one, they ... they'll recognise my name.'

'It won't be in your name, *ma chère*, that is what we have to arrange. By now you've become used to posing as Madame d'Argentière, and you will go out under that name.'

'I can't do that, Téo. The subterfuge may have worked on the natives here, and even deceived the Minister, but when it comes to papers and passports the authorities will need proof, a ... a marriage certificate, and a birth certificate . . . '

'You can ask your parents to send out a copy of the last, and I don't suppose the authorities will connect the estimable Perdita Cartwright with the young vagabond who slipped through their fingers at Casa. If they do, their filing system is very much better than I think it is and your original document will be mouldering in some office in Casa. The marriage certificate can be obtained.'

His smooth face was perfectly blank as he looked down at the table.

'How?' she demanded. 'Not . . . a forgery?'

'Certainly not. We can be married in Rabat or Tangier, there are English churches there.'

'We couldn't. According to Moslem law you can have two wives, but not by British. Besides . . . besides, if ever your wife got to hear of it, she'd be furious.'

A shadow crossed his face. 'She can't,' he said shortly. 'She's dead.'

Peta's universe seemed to rock around her. He had always spoken of Lucie as if she were still alive, concealing the fact that he was a widower. She felt a little stab of anger at the deception. Had he felt it necessary to put a barrier between them in their unconventional situation? Did he imagine that she would try to compromise him? Now, in his anxiety to send her home, he had not only come clean but was ready to go through a form of marriage with her to stabilise her position, which seemed a little inconsistent, but he never had been very consistent in his attitude towards her. It was another chivalrous impulse, she supposed, like his original rescue of her, and might lead to as many complications. Then, noticing the pain in his face, she exclaimed:

'I'm sorry.'

'I'd lost Lucie and the boy in an air crash,' he went on harshly, 'some five years ago. I'd gone to meet them at the airport.' His gaze was fixed on the opposite wall, recalling

121

the tragic scene, while he fumbled for his cigarettes. The trite phrase, 'How dreadful!' hovered on Peta's lips, but she did not utter the inadequate words, nor was he listening; momentarily she was forgotten. Téo's lighter flared, he drew deeply on his cigarette and returned it to his pocket. Peta's thoughts winged to that pathetic collection of children's clothes she had discovered. The box must have been sent out ahead of Lucie to await her coming to rejoin her husband. She wondered how Téo could have borne seeing her in one of the last dresses belonging to his wife, but the passage of the years might have dulled his grief.

'The Moslems accept such catastrophes fatalistically with their infernal *Insh' Allah*,' he said savagely. 'The Will of God! I cursed both God and man. He was only two years old, my little son.'

He fell into a brooding silence.

Peta's heart went out to him on a wave of pity that she could not express in words. Words were so futile, and he was not a man who would welcome condolences from strangers, and she was little more than that to him. A piece of flotsam washed up by the sea of life that he had salvaged and would in time float away from him.

'I met Lucie in Paris when I was on leave,' Téo began again, completely lost in his memories. 'It was what the novelists call a whirlwind courtship. Never trust infatuation, Perdita, it can't stand up to the ordinary stresses of life. She was enthralled by my accounts of Morocco, but when she got here, she hated it. Of course I didn't expect her to live at Dar el Bali. I took a bungalow for her in Marrakech and visited her whenever I could. She went north for Marcel's birth, where it was cooler. She stayed with the Daumiers. They have a house in Rabat as well as the estate in the Rif, but she didn't like it any better than Marrakech. She was for ever urging me to try for a job in France, but,' he smiled sadly, 'even if Grandpère had conveniently died then, I don't think she would have liked the Camargue any more than Africa. It was Paris, Paris all the time, and what could I do in Paris? Besides, I was interested in my job and didn't want to leave it.'

He became silent and Peta began to reconstruct what his married life must have been, the endless bickering between the frivolous daugher of Paris and the dedicated man of the desert.

'She had been on a visit to her parents,' Téo resumed, 'and I hadn't seen her for a month. She promised to come here for a few weeks, in the winter, of course, and I was eagerly looking forward to their arrival. I went to meet them at Casablanca and...'

His voice died away. So it was quite true that Lucie had never been to the oasis. Only her luggage had preceded her, that chest of dead memories that Téo had opened for Peta's benefit. She looked down at the dress she was wearing and thought it ought to have been a shroud.

Presently Téo sighed and looked at her with a wry smile.

'*Eh bien*, you see there's no just cause or impediment to our union,' he said lightly 'and a union it must be. I draw the line at forgery.'

'But won't it entail all sorts of formalities?'

'Nothing that can't be overcome with the help of a little palm oil, which is usual here. You needn't worry about anything, *ma chère*, leave it all to me.'

'You're very generous,' she declared with a break in her voice. There seemed no end to her obligations towards this man.

'Not at all. I'm merely proposing to make you respectable, which is a small return for the pleasure of your company,' he told her gallantly, and she feared insincerely. 'After I've been alone with you for so long I'm sure your parents will expect me to marry you.'

That she could not deny. Her own modern set would

think nothing of her present circumstances, even if there had been a liaison, but her parents were old-fashioned. She could well imagine her mother's horror if she ever learned exactly what had occurred.

'I should hate them to believe I was a villain,' Téo went on, watching her closely. 'I admire your father's writings and I should like to meet him some day, but with a clear conscience.'

'They needn't know anything about it.'

Téo pretended to look shocked. 'You would deceive them? Besides, someone is sure to talk.'

'I don't suppose it would get round to them, and when people won't move with the times, one just has to censor one's activities, unless one wants to hurt them, and that I don't like doing,' Peta explained, remembering Maud's disapproval of her excursion to Morocco with the three boys. 'I only soothed my mother's apprehensions about my holiday by telling her I was engaged to Keith, or more correctly, she assumed that I was and I let her think so.'

'The young man who proved such a broken reed?'

'He couldn't have done anything if I had appealed to him, which I don't suppose I should have been allowed to do.'

'But you still have a *tendresse* for him, and that is why you wish to remain faithful to him?'

'I never had a *tendresse* for him, as I've said before, and I owe him nothing,' Peta said vehemently, wondering why Téo persisted in harping upon Keith, whom she had barely mentioned.

He laughed. '*Bon*, then no fond memories need stand in your way. Be assured I intend that you shall leave Morocco without a stain upon your character. May I consider the matter settled?'

'No—please—I must think.' Though she had dreamed of being Téo's wife it was on the assumption that he loved her, not as an expediency, and she went on urgently, 'I don't see why you should burden yourself with me any further. I've caused you enough ... inconvenience as it is.'

He gave her an unexpectedly sweet smile.

'Your eyes are like Marcel's,' he said simply.

Marcel, not Lucie, and she divined that the child had been more to him than the wife. Since he frequently addressed her as *'mon enfant'* he must put her on a par with his two-year-old, and she aroused his protective instincts or some such, but she wanted to awake something much more adult.

'You're being sentimental,' she declared, 'and that's not a good enough reason for such quixoticism. You'd much better dump me on the British Consul in Rabat and perhaps he can help me out.'

'I refuse to dump you upon anyone,' Téo announced firmly. 'When I yielded to that somewhat rash impulse to hide you in my truck, I assumed responsibility for you.'

'I alone am responsible for myself,' she asserted.

He shook his head. 'Not after you came here. You might find it difficult to explain to your Consul why you didn't appeal to him in the first place, and it isn't only on the seaboard that smuggled goods arrive and leave the country. We're wide open to the lands beyond the desert down here, and your presence in Dar el Bali could be suspect. It's through this country the diamonds are carried. Besides, you wouldn't want to get me into trouble, would you?'

'God forbid, but why should you be?'

'For aiding and abetting your escape.'

Peta had not realised he was running a risk by doing that.

'Oh dear, and I never considered that,' she exclaimed contritely.

'I'm needed in France,' he told her earnestly. 'I don't want to be held in this country indefinitely while they sort me out in their peculiarly dilatory way. At best I should have to pay a heavy fine.'

Peta was silent, twisting her hands together. She certainly did not want to bring further trouble upon him, and to go through a form of marriage with him was a possible solution to their problems.

'Moreover, if there is an inquiry, the Minister might remember that he met you here as Madame d'Argentière, and that wouldn't look too good,' Téo went on insinuatingly.

'You insisted upon that,' she reminded him.

'Since I had this plan in mind, I wanted to see how you played your part.'

'You were testing me?'

'You passed with honours.'

Peta checked an indignant retort. He was within his rights. She had come to him looking like a vagabond wastrel and he had wanted to discover if she could behave like a lady.

'What is the difficulty?' Téo asked, watching her downcast face. 'Your impersonation was highly successful, so why hesitate to make it a reality? After what happened when you met the snake, I flatter myself I'm not obnoxious to you.'

She blushed furiously as she recalled his reception of her naïve outburst; the humiliation still smarted. Naturally after that he expected that he only had to beckon and she would fall at his feet like a ripe fruit. But her pride revolted, for at best she could only be another Zillah to him, and at worst he would only have contemptuous pity for her fatuous folly. She wanted his love, which as he had said himself was something very different from what he was offering. But that had been buried with Lucie and Marcel and she doubted she had the ability to resurrect it. Though she was sure of her feeling for him, this marriage would be a cold thing if it were not reciprocated.

She said uncertainly: 'Standing in for your wife is very

different from the actuality. I . . . I don't think I can.'

'Can what?' he asked sharply, and as she did not reply but hung her head shamefacedly, he continued:

'I shall not claim my marital rights, if that's what's frightening you. Once we're back in Europe the marriage can be dissolved if you so wish. I know I'm somewhat old and shop-soiled,' he smiled wryly, '. . . to match your shining youth. So that could be the right solution.' As she still did not speak, he added, 'As for that little lapse the other day, I'm sorry I referred to it, since it obviously offended you. I promise you nothing of that kind shall occur again, and you can trust me.'

Even while he made this declaration, his expression softened and there was a questioning look in his eyes, almost an appeal, but Peta did not see it. Unable to meet his eyes, she was looking anywhere but at him. She interpreted his words to mean that though he was willing to give her the protection of his name, he would prefer the marriage to be a temporary measure.

'That puts a different complexion on the matter.' She forced a little laugh. 'So long as neither of us need feel bound . . .' She left the sentence hanging in mid-air.

'Far from it, and so long as the marriage isn't consummated, it can soon be annulled.'

'I understand.' Then because she was wounded by this indifference, and her pride was still affronted, she told him:

'The . . . er . . . arrangement could only be possible if you refrain from . . . er . . . intimacies.'

He eyed her with a curious wistfulness, even while he reproved her:

'That was an unnecessary thrust, *mon enfant*. Because I forgot myself once it doesn't mean I'll force my attentions upon you if they are not wanted.' He paused, but she gave no sign. How, she wondered drearily, did he account for her instantaneous response? Possibly he believed it had been unwillingly aroused, and she was now ashamed of it, as indeed she was.

'*Eh bien*,' he went on with a shrug, 'in a more temperate climate my manners will improve. The desert man will become a gentleman again.'

Impulsively she blurted out: 'I like you as you are.'

'Just now you indicated that you didn't like me at all.'

'I didn't mean that ... I mean...' She became incoherent.

He watched her, smiling a little sadly.

'I understand, you'd prefer a father figure to a husband. Also you're still a little blinded by the romance of the desert. In Europe you'll discover I am well past my first youth and be thankful we're not bound irrevocably. Lucie found me dull and resented my enthusiasm for work, and the *mas* will absorb me. You need not fear I shall make any demands upon you.' His face cleared and he laughed gaily. 'At least you will not have the audacity to play the jealous wife, will you?'

'Far from it,' she declared, stung by his attitude. 'You can have as many Zillahs as you fancy!'

A thought struck her. 'But since you've been free for ... how long is it, five years, why didn't you marry her?'

'Can you imagine Madame Sancé living here?' he inquired with a grin. 'If Zillah decides to wed again she will look out for a richer man than I. Meanwhile we both enjoy our liberty.'

Again Peta felt stung. Téo would not have proposed this marriage with her if he had thought it would be any threat to his freedom. Assuming a brightness she was far from feeling, she said lightly,

'Then it's a good thing ours is to be only a marriage of convenience and of short duration. I'll go straight home from Morocco and leave you to get on with your farming.'

To her surprise he looked disappointed.

'Won't you at least pay a short visit to my new heritage? It's a fascinating place. I stayed there as a boy—white horses, black bulls, and water, lagoons and rivers, delightful to contemplate in this dried-up land. I can promise you some good riding, my beautiful Amazon.'

'Oh, I'd love to see it,' she exclaimed. She had heard of the Camargue and its unique scenery, and Téo must indeed be carried away by the prospect if he had called her beautiful.

'*Vraiment?*'

She knew she would be unwise to go, the longer she stayed with Téo, the harder it would be to leave him, but she could not forgo this opportunity he was offering to her. Perhaps in a new environment she might come to view him differently and she was only suffering from an infatuation incited by the desert air. Then the inevitable parting would not be painful after all.

'I can't resist it,' she sighed.

'Why should you? Perhaps you'll hate it, it's not everybody's choice. It hasn't got the glamour of the Riviera, for instance.'

'That's in its favour. I don't care for the sophisticated glitter of smart resorts.'

'Have you ever been to one?' he asked.

'No, but I've read about them.'

'Then don't underestimate their attractions. Blue skies, blue sea and purple velvet nights. Mimosa in the spring, roses and carnations in the summer. Old villages and castles perched on precarious summits in the interior, redolent of history. I spent my honeymoon near Nice in a whitewashed villa mantled with bougainvillea and honeysuckle.'

Lucie the gay Parisienne would have appreciated that. Though she had died her memory lingered on. Peta sensed from Téo's faraway look that that honeymoon had been a time of rapture, whatever frictions developed later on, a rapture she would never experience herself, for he had made it plain that she would be no more than a guest in his home.

Although she had been frequently warned not to despise the strength of the sun and to remain in doors at midday, Peta's inner turmoil made her restless so that on the day following Téo's astonishing proposal, she went wandering down to the reservoir feeling cramped and stifled in the confines of the house. Téo was away for the day, and when he returned in the evening he found her with a blinding headache and a rapidly mounting temperature.

'Been out in the sun without a hat?' he inquired.

She looked at him glassy eyed. 'I wore my d'jellaba.'

'And pushed the hood back, I'll wager. You've got heat-stroke, *mon enfant*.'

'I . . . I must lie down.' She stumbled from the room, and that was her last coherent utterance for many days. She did not know where she was and thought she was back with her three companions in Fez.

'Keith, do keep an eye on Osric,' she muttered to Téo, 'he's up to something, I'm sure.' And she rambled on about contraband, kif, and her uneasy suspicions.

Téo scoured the country to obtain ice for her, raiding the hotels in Ouarzazate, and brought out a loudly complaining doctor, who told him he was crazy to bring his wife to a place like Dar el Bali in the summer. He left a supply of opiates and other drugs, and instructions for nursing which Meriem was quite incapable of carrying out. Moreover, she was deeply suspicious of Western medicines. The duty devolved upon Téo, who sponged Peta's feverish body night and morning, administered the dosages and coaxed her to accept liquid nourishment. For the most part she was unaware of his presence, but when she was she confused him with Keith, one night when he had completed his ministrations and given her a sedative, she seized his hand and said fervently:

'You've been wonderful, Keith, and I'll never love anyone but you.' Her eyelashes descended upon her flushed cheeks, and with some confused memory of Osric, she went on: 'It was always you, not that other one. Come and take me home out of this furnace, Keith, please, please!'

Téo stroked the hair back from her burning forehead and laid an ice-bag on it. His face was grim; her apparent obsession with Keith Morris indicated that she had deceived him when she had declared he meant nothing to her.

Lucie's flimsy nightwear was worn to shreds with continued washing. Meriem had no idea how to deal with such materials, her methods were primitive. Téo slept with both their doors ajar so that he would hear if Peta woke in the night, as she often did, for her sleep was but fitful, and he was instantly at her side when she began to ramble incoherently. It was reported in the village that El Sidi was the most devoted of husbands, though his *lallah* had not yet proved her worth by giving him a son.

At long last came a time when she slept the whole night through and woke to a falling temperature and sanity.

'Téo!' she exclaimed, pulling the sheet up to her chin as he came in soft-footed carrying a thermometer. 'Have I been ill?'

'Yes, *mon enfant*, but thanks to *le bon dieu* you seem to be on the mend. Let us prove it.' He put the instrument into her mouth.

Peta looked round the room, noticing the signs of invalid apparatus with her level brows knitted. When she could speak, she asked anxiously:

'Who had to look after me?'

'Never you mind,' he returned, reading the mercury. 'Yes, it's nearly normal. As soon as you're well enough to travel I must get you away up north, this climate's been too much for you.'

But she was not to be diverted.

'Did you have to nurse me?'

He looked uncomfortable.

'*Bien sûr*. As you can imagine, Meriem wasn't much use.'

'Oh dear, I'm never anything but a nuisance to you,' she sighed.

'*Tiens*, don't start worrying about that now or you'll send your temperature up again,' he said gruffly. Then with a sudden flash of irritation, 'You needn't fiddle with that sheet, it's been my privileged chore to bathe you daily.'

'Oh no!'

'Oh yes, but it doesn't matter, you're soon to be my legal wife and you have a very beautiful body. Unfortunately this illness of yours has rather held me up, but I've written to your parents.'

'But you didn't know their address.'

'I obtained it from that boy-friend of yours, whose name you've been muttering every half hour. You told me he elected to stay in Fez, and the British Council put me in touch with him. Incidentally, he sends you his love.' Téo's voice was very dry.

'That's merely a *façon de parler*, but I don't know why I had him on my mind,' said Peta.

'That's a question only you can answer.'

'But . . .' she was too weak to puzzle further. 'Oh, Téo, I can never repay you for all you've done,' she whispered tearfully.

'You can do that by obeying me implicitly for your own good. Ismael is bringing you some breakfast which I hope you'll eat. Then you must sleep again. You're to get well as quickly as possible so that we can get on with the tiresome formalities that have to be gone through to enable me to take you to a more suitable environment.'

From his tone she deduced that something had occurred to incense him, and she wondered vaguely if Keith had been tactless, and surely there was no harm in sending his love? It was what most people would say when a friend was ill, and he felt no more for her than the fraternal affection that she returned. She was quite unaware that she had given a wrong impression during her delirium.

Ismael came to her door with a tray which Téo took from him to place beside her. On it was cereal and tinned peaches, unusual fare for Dar el Bali.

'Purloined from the Hotel du Sud,' Téo told her with a wry smile, 'together with some meat jelly and other delicacies. We've no stores of invalid food here.'

'Oh, Téo!' Her eyes filled with tears. 'You spoil me, and I . . .' Her voice broke.

'*Pour l'amour de dieu*, don't upset yourself,' he exclaimed in consternation. 'I did no more than any humane person would do for a sick child. Eat your breakfast and then you'll feel better.'

She did feel better, and from that morning onwards, being young and healthy, she made good progress. But the enervating heat and its culmination had taken their toll of her strength and she continued to suffer from lassitude. It was an effort to exert herself—not that there was any need to do so, for Téo took complete control of her life, prescribing what she should eat and drink and when she should rest. His solicitude would have been very sweet to her if it had not been accompanied by an increasing aloofness, for though his care for her physical well-being was constant, he never talked to her intimately if he could help it and he ceased her Arabic lessons, saying she was not well enough to study and he had no time. He was, she knew, very busy with preparations for his departure and correspondence in connection with his heritage and also their marriage.

No reply had yet come from her parents, but the posts

were slow, and one evening she asked him a little anxiously what he had said to them.

'Why, that we were getting married, of course, and we proposed to live in France. Incidentally, I told them you were a little indisposed but would write when you were feeling better, so you'd better do so. The story is that you wandered as far as Ouarzazate where we met and I offered to show you the country. If you want to tell them the true story, you'd better do it yourself.'

'No, I should hate them to know what really happened,' Peta said slowly. 'I'm sorry you told them about ... about the marriage. Couldn't you have thought of another excuse for needing the certificate?'

She was thinking that when in due course she returned to London it would be easier if they did not know she had been married.

'No, I could not,' he said firmly. 'They had a right to know. I don't care for underhand nonsense. You weren't straight about that youth you came out with, but you're going to be with your parents.'

She supposed he was referring to Keith and wondered what the boy could have said to raise his ire, but she shrank from his biting tone, and let the matter drop.

As soon as she was judged strong enough to travel, Téo told her he had chartered a private plane to fly them over the mountains to Marrakech from whence they would take the train to Rabat.

Peta was not used to hiring planes and she gasped, 'Won't it be terribly expensive?'

'It's necessary, you aren't fit to cross the Atlas by road. I'm not a pauper and our mutual friend the Minister is helping with my moving expenses. He's very relieved that I'm leaving without any fuss and he was sorry to hear that the climate has avenged itself upon my "courageous" spouse.'

Again his voice was dry, as it so often was when he spoke to her now, and Peta wilted inwardly.

'Shall we stay at a hotel in Rabat?' she inquired.

'I shall, but you can't without a passport. I told you the Daumiers have a house in that city and Yvette has kindly offered to put you up for the necessary period. They're in residence there now.' He laughed cynically. 'She was very surprised to hear I was going to get married again.'

Peta's heart sank. She had not liked what she had seen of Yvette Daumier, and she did not think she would be sympathetic towards any woman whom Téo favoured.

'Before you go there we must shop,' Téo went on. 'You can't appear before Yvette in Lucie's clothes.'

'Did she ... did she know her?' Peta faltered, feeling Yvette would be still more surprised when she met Téo's supposed choice of the beautiful Lucie's successor.

'Naturally, didn't I tell you we were old friends?'

Peta had a sensation of being trapped. The situation was becoming more and more impossible. Téo objected to deceit, but her position was entirely false as this was not to be a real marriage, but she lacked the strength to protest or seek another way out. She was fairly certain from his changed attitude towards her that Téo was regretting his quixotic action, but was doggedly persisting with it because he could not think what else to do with her.

When it came to saying goodbye to Dar el Bali she nearly wept; tears came all too easily since she had been ill. The place had been a sanctuary for her and there she had fallen in love and spent many happy hours in Téo's company. Ismael and Meriem were obviously grieved by their departure, though they accepted it with the stoicism of their creed, and called down blessings upon their heads. Blessings which I shall need, Peta thought, for she dreaded going to Rabat to be the guest of the Daumiers, who were not her friends. It was an ordeal that must be endured, but when it was over and Téo had taken her to France, was there a remote chance that he might turn towards her and make their union a genuine one? He had seemed eager for her to visit the place, and he might feel lonely at first. Moreover, in the Carmargue there would be no memories of Lucie and the boy, while Peta would be in her right element. She was good with horses and enjoyed country life, which she divined Lucie had not, for she would have hated the Camargue as much as she had hated Morocco. Propinquity and mutual interests might work a miracle if she were able to stay there long enough.

So through the gloom of her present perplexities, hope ran like a golden thread and sustained her through the last sad farewells to Dar el Bali.

# CHAPTER EIGHT

THE Daumiers owned a beautiful house in the modern part of Rabat. It was built Spanish style round a central patio with a fountain and a profusion of flowers and shrubs. Peta arrived hot, dusty and tired after the long train journey and Téo insisted that she must go to bed after having a bath. She was conducted to a cool tiled room with windows opening on to the colonnade of Moorish arches surrounding the patio, to which its own bathroom was attached.

Yvette and her husband Gustave had greeted her hospitably. He was a dapper little Frenchman with a horsey look, but when Téo suggested a bath and supper in bed for his fiancée, who, he explained, had not been well, Yvette leaped at the suggestion with alacrity, seeing a chance to get Téo to herself. Peta was too exhausted to care. Next morning coffee and fresh rolls were brought to her by a Moroccan maid with the information that Monsieur and Madame would be in the patio if she cared to join them later on. Appreciative of the luxury of the house after the austerity of the desert, Peta took another bath and with reviving spirits dressed herself in one of the new outfits Téo had bought for her in Marrakech. She would have much preferred trousers and a tank top, but he had insisted upon a dress.

She went out into the patio where she found her hosts seated in canvas chairs under a huge umbrella. Gustave sprang up as she approached and ushered her to a seat, and proceeded to pay her insincere compliments, while Yvette studied her insolently, secretly wondering whatever Téo could see in this tall thin girl with her apathetic manner, for

Peta had not yet recovered her former vigour. She had to rouse herself to parry her hostess's questions, for Yvette wanted to know when and where she had met Téo and how she happened to be in Dar el Bali, which she understood was hell on earth in the summer and it was not surprising she had got heat-stroke.

Peta admitted that it had been very hot, but it was the only opportunity she had had to see that part of the country and she had been staying at Ouarzazate when she had run into Téo collecting material for one of her father's books, which was a little embroidery on the story Téo had concocted.

'But you can't have known him long,' Yvette said bluntly.

'Well, he has to go back to France and there didn't seem much point in waiting.'

'*Vraiment*, that is so when one is young and in love,' Gustave agreed gallantly.

'But all the same it's rather rash to rush into marriage,' Yvette observed spitefully. 'That is the main cause of so many divorces, the young people have not had a chance to really come to know each other. Besides, you have no time to make preparations.'

'We don't need to make any,' Peta returned coldly, resenting the other woman's impertinence. 'There's everything waiting for us at the *mas*.'

'And naturally Téo would not want to go there alone,' Gustave said. 'His grandfather's sudden death precipitated matters, *n'est-ce pas?*'

Peta smiled wanly. 'It did.'

Yvette was still curious, but her husband tactfully guided the conversation on to other matters. He described his estate in the Rif and his horses. Peta did not mention that she had been in the locality and she wondered what Madame would have said if she announced that she had been present at her first meeting with Téo, when she had re-covered Mustapha.

Téo came in during the morning and Yvette, who had been looking bored, became vivacious. Gustave clapped his hands for a servant to bring drinks and the conversation became French and animated. Peta noticed Téo looking at her with a wry smile and an odd expression in his eyes. She sensed that something unexpected had occurred, but he did not want to speak before the Daumiers.

She began to wonder if there had been a hitch in his arrangements with an unco-operative officialdom, or was he having second thoughts and had dreamed up another way to dispose of her?

At last Gustave rose, saying he had some correspondence which needed his attention, and glanced meaningly at his wife.

'I am sure Téo and Mademoiselle Cartwright have much to say to each other.'

'Her name is Perdita,' Téo told him.

'Perdeeta? *C'est jolie.* Come, Yvette.'

Peta, who was nearest to her, heard her mutter in French, 'The only pretty thing about her,' as she unwill-ingly stood up. She smiled at Téo. 'You will stay for *déjeuner*?'

'Thank you, I will. Perdita should take it easy today, but tomorrow I'll take her off your hands.'

'But we like to entertain her here,' Gustave protested, and Yvette added with her eyes on Téo,

'And you too, *mon ami.*'

She still lingered, until her husband drew her arm through his and marched her away.

Peta said disdainfully, for Yvette had ruffled her, 'Your lady friends stick like limpets.'

'Poor Yvette, she never stops trying,' Téo returned care-lessly. Then he looked at Peta sternly. 'Get this clear—I don't betray my friends, and Gustave is my friend.'

'Your scruples do you credit,' Peta declared with a slight edge to her voice, 'but isn't it a little cruel to inflict me upon her, although I don't think she considers me to be a serious rival.'

'There's no question of rivalry,' he told her stiffly.

'Just what I said—but what have you to tell me? There is something, isn't there?'

Again the wry smile. 'I'm not sure of it's good news or bad. I told your parents where I would be staying, and they've cabled to say they're coming out for the wedding.'

'Oh, lord!' She stared at him in dismay. 'They aren't going to forbid the banns or whatever it is we have to have?'

'Far from it, they've posted the certificate. This personal descent upon us is an afterthought.'

'Well, you would tell them, so you've only yourself to blame.'

'From which I deduce you consider it's bad news? Aren't you an unnatural daughter!'

'Oh, Téo,' she burst out, 'if it were a normal wedding...'

'But it will be a normal wedding,' he interrupted her. 'We'll lay on a church service for their benefit and it will all be perfectly legal. Nothing they can take exception to.'

She looked down into her lap, twisting her fingers together. She could anticipate her mother's tearful sentimentality, her father's searching questions, and she did not think she could endure them.

'I expect they'll approve of you,' she said dully, for they would be immensely curious to learn how she had managed to acquire such a suitable partner, which meant she would have to exercise considerable evasion.

'Are they then so difficult to please?' he asked.

'Well, I told you they don't think much of my student friends.'

140

His eyes glinted. 'They'll be thankful it isn't Keith Morris?'

'You always have to come back to him,' she said wearily. 'Surely he didn't suggest he had any claim on me when you contacted him?'

'No. As far as he's concerned I'm satisfied it's over.'

He emphasised the 'he', which would indicate that he thought Keith meant something to her.

'There wasn't anything to get over,' she protested firmly.

'Don't pretend, I appreciate honesty. You raved about him all the time you were ill.'

'When I didn't know what I was saying. I must have confused him with—— Oh, it doesn't matter.' Peta noticed his look of unbelief. For some obscure reason he wanted to convince himself she was yearning for the other man. Then she laughed. 'It's a pity you can't see him, then you'd realise he's a mere child.'

'And so are you.'

She turned her head away, her lips quivering. Would he ever see her as a woman?

'Fortunately I'm fond of children,' he observed, and sighed.

She knew he was thinking of Marcel, but he could have another son if he made their marriage a reality. She wondered if she dared to hint it, but his face had the closed, forbidding look it always wore when he recalled his loss, so she did not speak. Perhaps he thought she was too juvenile to bear his sons.

He cut into her reflections with prosaic remarks about accommodation for her parents. Not at his hotel, he decided, but one at a distance.

'Though I'll show them round. I don't want them infringing too far upon my last days of bachelor freedom,' he said jocularly.

Peta looked at him speculatively. He already looked

better than during the last days at Dar el Bali, younger, the lines of care smoothed from his face. She wondered what exact form of relaxation he had sought, and then was ashamed of her suspicion.

'You'll soon be free again,' she suggested tentatively.

Téo gave her an enigmatical look.

'I consider it rather bad form to discuss the ending of a marriage before it has begun,' he drawled.

Again the golden thread of hope wove through her thoughts. Could he mean he did not want an anulment after all?

The Cartwrights duly arrived and Téo went to meet them alone. Their plane was due in at midday and he said Peta should not stand about in the heat. For the first time she blessed her illness; it would be much easier to meet her parents after he had broken the ice. She was sure that they would be agreeably surprised by his appearance and personality and consider she was lucky to have captured him. If only she had!

He took her to their hotel for dinner that same evening, telling her en route that he had explained everything to them satisfactorily.

'Naturally they imagine it was a whirlwind romance,' he told her drily, 'and I didn't undeceive them. I like your father immensely. Your mother——' he gave a Gallic shrug. 'I'm afraid you'll have to endure a flood of sentimental mush.'

'Poor Mummy,' Peta sighed. 'She finds her emotional outlet in vicarious romances.'

'Don't you dare to disillusion her,' he warned.

'Oh, I won't.' The last thing she wanted was for Maud to discover the true state of affairs.

Téo laid himself out to be charming over dinner. He glossed over the facts leading to Peta's arrival in the deep south, saying she had left her companions because they did

142

not wish to travel so far and she wanted to traverse the Atlas. He had arranged a lodging for her in the oasis. Knowing where that lodging had been, Peta smiled inwardly and hoped her parents would not ask for details.

They did not, Maud because she considered all Peta's actions incomprehensible and Timothy because mention of the Anti Atlas set him off on a spate of eager questions about kasbahs and geological formations.

During the days that followed both parents expressed their approval of Peta's fiancé. Timothy said he was a practical and intelligent man and he had never dared to hope his harum-scarum daughter would make such a wise choice. Maud was relieved to discover that he was not one of the avant-garde types she disliked so much, that he shaved, cut his hair and had charming manners. Moreover, he seemed competent to control Peta's waywardness.

She was shocked to find that Peta was contemplating matrimony without a proper outfit and whisked her off to purchase a miniature trousseau.

'Though with this hole-and-corner arrangement you won't get any wedding presents,' she complained. 'They're such a help when setting up house.'

'Téo has got a home already equipped,' Peta pointed out, feeling a fraud. 'We shan't need anything.'

With this return to normal life the circumstances that had led up to her engagement no longer seemed relevant, for with her father there to protect her, the necessity for such an extreme measure disappeared. Surely Timothy could procure an exit visa for her by explaining that she had lost her passport? Officials would listen to him with respect. It was not fair to Téo to make him go through with it when he need not do so.

It was some time before she could being herself to broach the subject to him, because with the arrival of the Cartwrights she rarely saw him alone; either they or the Daumiers were present and Téo made no effort to detach her from them; moreover, she was very reluctant to break the bond between them. He was always courteous and pleasant when they met, but he seemed to be withdrawing further from her every day; there was no real intimacy between them and he never spoke of either his future or hers. Anyone less like an ardent bridegroom it was difficult to imagine. It was this detached attitude of his that strengthened Peta's resolution to release him in spite of her disinclination. The thought of parting was desolation, and any sort of connection was better than none, but she decided she could not impose upon his good nature any longer.

She asked him to take her to the Kasbah des Oudaias, for there was little chance of privacy in Yvette's house.

'I've heard it's delightful, and I've never been there,' she said gaily.

He had called at the Daumiers' and been monopolised by Gustave, but Peta managed to waylay him on his way out.

'I'm very busy. Won't your father take you?'

His reluctance was painfully obvious, but she persisted.

'I want you, Téo, and I must speak to you alone,' she insisted urgently as she heard the tap of Yvette's heels approaching along the marble paving. 'Call for me tomorrow morning, about eleven, please!'

'Very well,' he agreed, and she slipped away as Madame Daumier hailed him eagerly.

The Kasbah des Oudaias was a beautiful Moorish garden enclosed by high walls and entered by a fine gateway. It had once been a fort guarding the river which it overlooked. Storks nested on top of the old ramparts, the big black and white birds with their scarlet bills and legs giving a decorative touch as they perched on their untidy nests. In one corner was a Moorish café and there Téo and Peta sat down and ordered glasses of mint tea.

'*Eh bien,* what is this urgent matter?' Téo asked as their

brew was set before them. He was watching the storks with a great deal more interest than he was showing in her.

'Simply that I want to call the whole thing off,' she said in a breathless rush. 'It isn't necessary, as I'm sure Dad can get me out of Morocco and I can go home with him.'

Téo turned in his seat and stared at her, his eyes blazing like yellow flame.

'*Mon dieu, ma fille*, but I didn't think you were a quitter.'

This reaction was unexpected, but she went on bravely:

'But, Téo, you must see...'

'No, I do not see,' he interrupted. His hand shot out and gripped her wrist like an iron fetter. 'Do you know what I've been through, using bribery and cajolery on your account? If your father can help you, why didn't you apply to him in the first place and save me all the trouble I've taken? Right from the start you've used me, expecting me to get you out of Casa and shield you from the consequences of your folly. Now you think you can do without me, you want to drop me, but when we part—if we part,' his grip tightened until she thought her bones would crack, 'it'll be in my time, not in yours. It's about time you showed me some consideration. If you back out now what are the Daumiers going to say? What excuse can you give your parents? Do you mean to tell them the whole story? How you posed as a boy, slept with me, lived with me—they'll find it edifying.'

He spoke with passionate vehemence, his lean brown fingers all but breaking her wrist.

'No, oh no!' she gasped. 'I couldn't do that, but ... but ... people have been known to decide they've made a mistake at the last moment. I could say I found I wasn't in love with you.'

'You never have been.' Was there a tinge of bitterness in

his tone?

'But I told you...' she coloured vividly. 'After the snake...'

'That wasn't love, that was a moment of teenage infatuation. You don't know what real love is. I do.' Lucie, she thought despairingly. 'But you're not going to back out now. You'll marry me if I have to drag you to the altar!'

He released her wrist and she rubbed it mechanically. There would be a bruise where it had been maltreated, but she did not care. She was jubilant that her offer had been rejected. She did not know what was motivating him, a fear of outraged conventionalism if all was disclosed, a dislike of opposition, a tyrannical desire to impose his will upon a rebel, it might be any of these things, it might even be that he still needed her company. If only she could eradicate the memory of Lucie she might win him yet. Meanwhile there was still hope.

In the tense silence that fell between them the clapping of the storks' bills was clearly audible and distracted her attention.

'I thought they always went to Europe to breed,' she remarked, while she tried to order her seething thoughts.

'Some of them are permanent residents,' Téo told her abstractedly. 'Their numbers have been decimated since the introduction of poison spray to kill the locusts on which they feed. More victims of progress.'

'What a shame!' But Peta was too preoccupied by her own troubles to spare much sympathy for the storks. Téo was a little cruel to dismiss her feelings so carelessly as a teenage infatuation. Even so he should know that youthful crushes could be painful. Lucie could not have been much older when he had married her, but being a sophisticated Parisienne she would have known how to intrigue a man, and how to hold him when she had got him. She still held Téo even after death. Peta sighed; she herself was too straightforward, too brash, she had no subtlety, and so Téo did not believe in the genuineness of her emotions.

Téo drained his glass of tea. His passion had faded though he still looked stern.

'*Eh bien, mon enfant*, are you going to be reasonable?' he asked.

'I suppose I must do as you say,' she agreed, refusing to accept that it was reasonable, 'but need I come with you to the Camargue?'

'What option have you?' he returned. 'Naturally you'll be expected to go away with me. You can't possibly return home with your parents.'

This was not quite the answer she had hoped for, but his next words were more encouraging:

'What has changed you? I thought you were keen to come.'

She hesitated, it was his indifference that had wounded her.

'I do want to ... to see the place,' she admitted, 'but how long will I have to be there?'

He eyed her implacably. 'You will stay as long as I wish you to do so.'

She laughed a little uneasily. Something in his tone scared her. It sounded almost brutal.

'You grow more despotic every day, Téo. It's the Eastern influence, I suppose.'

'Don't talk rubbish,' he said sharply. Then he relaxed. '*Eh bien, mon enfant*, you will need time to consider what you're going to do next.' He smiled. 'This ... er ... interlude will have interrupted your training schedule, *n'est-ce pas*? But I've no wish to deprive the world of a future Olympic champion.'

Was he laughing at her? She was not sure. His smooth brown face expressed only urbane inquiry. The moment of violence had vanished completely, but her aching wrist bore testimony that it had been.

She said despondently: 'My illness has put paid to all that.'

'Nonsense. You'll soon recover your vigour. I'm looking forward to applauding your career from the sidelines.'

But that was not what Peta wanted now. All that running and jumping seemed foolishly juvenile. She saw the brilliant flowers in the garden through a sudden mist of tears.

'What's the matter?' Téo demanded impatiently. 'You are the most unpredictable creature, Perdita. Here was I thinking everything was settled to your satisfaction and you have to try to upset the applecart. What *do* you want?'

Your love—the words nearly escaped her, but she bit them back. Had Téo any love to give, or was it buried with Lucie and Marcel?

She managed a watery smile. 'I'm sorry, Téo, but I'm a woman, not a ... boy or a child, and women, you must know, are changeable.'

'I'll be obliged if you'll refrain from practising your developing femininity on me,' he said sharply, and with difficulty she checked a rush of tears. She was sure he never spoke to Zillah or Yvette as he did to her, however aggravating they were. Why then was he so harsh with her?

'*Enfin*,' he went on more kindly; 'you've had a rough time, but it is unlike my Amazon to be so weepy. *Courage, mon enfant*, bear up for a little longer and then you can relax among the reeds and lagoons of your new home.'

Home? She caught at the word as a drowning man clutches at a straw. Would it really prove to be a home to her? But he had called her an Amazon and a child, which was not how she wished to appear to him.

'Now if you've said all you wish to say, and most of it has been better unsaid, do you feel equal to climbing the Tour Hassan? The view from the top is worth the exertion.'

148

Peta assented eagerly; she would endure any ordeal to keep him with her, nor did she tell him she had been up the tower on her former visit. Actually the climb was not very formidable, as like many Moorish edifices there were no steps, only a spiral ramp.

Their route to the tower followed the course of the river, and passed through several streets of shops. Peta recovered her spirits and chattered brightly about all they saw. In the street of the carpet-sellers she paused to admire one of the special designs for which Rabat was famous and Téo decided he would buy it for the *mas*. Then followed the usual bargaining, at which he was adept. A satisfactory price was reached and instructions given for its despatch.

'Though I don't know how it's going to fit into the Provençal décor,' he remarked as they proceeded along the street.

'Téo, you didn't buy it because I admired it?' she asked anxiously.

'I thought you would like a memento of Africa in our home.'

Again he had spoken of home. It has a pleasant permanent sound, and so elated her that she was able to walk up the ramp of the tower with something of her old vigour.

From its top they could see over the river to the white houses of Salé, once a nest of pirates that had threatened even Rabat's security. Planes ascended and descended from its airport. Southwards they could see as far as the cultivated lands and woods beyond the environments of the town, but Téo kept his gaze on the airport.

'In a few more days we'll be flying from there,' he told her. 'I'm longing to get to the *mas*.'

'You've no regrets for Dar el Bali?'

'Regrets are a waste of time,' he returned. 'That part of my life is over. Always look forward, *mon enfant*.'

Peta wondered if that would apply to Lucie and the

child; she hoped so, but people were less easily forgotten than places, people who had been loved.

Maud Cartwright's romantic soul yearned for a white bridal gown and veil, but about that Peta put her foot down. The ceremony was to be as simple as possible and nobody was going to dress up. She chose a severely cut blue two-piece in uncrushable linen and a straw hat, thankful that she could pay for her clothes herself, as her father had given her a substantial cheque for a wedding present.

On the last night Maud, mindful of her maternal duty, took her into her bedroom and said bashfully:

'I suppose you know all about it, darling? You ... er ... don't want to ask me anything?'

'It's all right, Mummy. It would be difficult to be ignorant nowadays,' Peta told her drily.

She had an impulse to confide in her mother and pour out the whole story, also the humiliating confession that no wedding night would follow the nuptial rites, but Maud was looking so relieved that she was not to be called upon to make any embarrassing disclosures that the impulse died. They had never been close, the generation gap between them was too great, and she would be dismayed to learn that her daughter was not making a love match. Téo had commanded Peta not to disillusion her, and he was right. So the opportunity for greater intimacy between them passed and would never come again.

Morning came and Peta went through the motions of becoming Téo's wife in name at least, and the proceedings were like a dream. She moved and spoke like an automaton. Téo, unfamiliar in a dark suit, seemed almost a stranger. Only the Daumiers and the Cartwrights were present at both the civil and the church ceremonies. Afterwards they had a meal together at a restaurant, during which Maud became tearful at the imminent parting from the daughter she rarely saw. The two couples accompanied the bridal pair to Salé to see them off on their flight to Marseilles.

At the barrier, Téo presented their joint passport with a flourish, and when it had been duly scrutinised and they had gone through into the departure lounge, he turned to Peta with his old familiar grin and said:

'Mission accomplished.'

He had got her out of Morocco as he had promised, but what of the other promises he had made earlier in the day? Did they mean anything to him?

Peta could only wonder.

# CHAPTER NINE

It was evening when the newly married pair reached Mas d'Argentière, and it had been raining. The sky was covered by a pall of grey cloud broken near the horizon to show a glimpse of lemon sunset. The country was flat and desolate, rivers and lagoons reflecting the pewter sky, the sentinel reeds that fringed them turning brown with the approach of autumn's chill.

To Peta it looked sad and depressing, but Téo was jubilant.

'I haven't seen a day like this for years,' he told her, and she remembered what he had said about grey being a soft refreshing colour and after the harsh sunlight of the desert he was revelling in the contrast, but for her it was a little too great.

'I suppose the sun does shine here sometimes,' she remarked, for her ideas about the South of France were coloured in azure and gold.

'Oh, frequently, and it is hot in the summer, but the autumn can be wet and stormy.'

They were driving in a hired car which Téo had ordered to meet them at the airport outside Marseilles. The chauffeur sat stolidly in front of them, divided from them by a glass screen so that he could not hear their conversation.

'Will there be anyone at the Mas to receive us?' Peta asked. 'I believe you said your grandfather had a house-keeper.'

'Yes, a Madame Boulanger, and although he left her a pension, she has agreed to stay on for the time being. I've been in communication with her and she seems to be a competent body, and we shall need her services, for we both have a lot to learn before we take over.'

He spoke as if she were going to be a permanency, and Peta forbore to mention that there would not be much point in learning to run the Mas if she were soon to leave it. Perhaps she could succeed in making herself indispensable, though that seemed to be an unlikely possibility, and then she would never have to leave. She glanced at the man sitting beside her who unbelievably was technically her husband. She was far from his mind at that moment; leaning forward in his seat, he was gazing raptly at the marshy land they were traversing and all she could see of his face was his eagle profile. Since they had landed in France he had seemed much younger, almost a boy again in his eager anticipation. Fervently she hoped that the ranch would come up to his expectations and he would not be disappointed.

The 'competent body' was standing in the lighted doorway to greet them as they drove up to the Mas. It was a low, roomy house, built to withstand winter storms and the mistral's force, with a windbreak of cypress trees to protect it on the north, on which side of the house there were no windows. Though it was not yet dark, the lights had been turned on to dispel the gloom of the dismal day and Peta saw with relief that the place was furnished with electricity.

'*Monsieur! Madame!*' The woman bobbed a kind of curtsey. 'Welcome! Georges will bring in your luggage. You have had a good journey, yes?'

Her inquisitive dark eyes were assessing them boldly, though her words were deferential. She was a comely woman of about forty, wearing a flower printed overall over her dress. She had black hair drawn back into a knot in her nape, which from its size indicated it was plentiful, and she had the classic features often met with in Provence. But her fine eyes held a hard, calculating expression which Peta

153

found displeasing. She decided she was not at all her idea of a cosy housekeeper.

While they exchanged pleasantries, Peta noticed the quizzical gleam in Téo's eyes and knew he was amused by the contradictions that Madame Boulanger's appearance presented, she hoped he did not admire her.

'I have prepared your rooms,' Madame told them. 'The guest room also, as requested.' She looked beyond them for the guest.

Téo vouchsafed no explanation and, Georges having decanted their cases, paid off the driver. As Madame Boulanger ushered them upstairs to show them to their rooms he whispered to Peta in English:

'I applaud my grandfather's taste in housekeepers.'

So he did admire her.

'She's a little too ornamental for her position, isn't she?' Peta said sourly.

Téo shrugged his shoulders. 'Need she be a drab? I like nice-looking people around me.'

A cold shiver of presentiment ran down Peta's spine, and she hoped Madame Boulanger would not want to stay much longer at the Mas.

The housekeeper threw open a door at the head of the stairs.

'The master bedroom.'

Like all the rooms·in the house it had a polished wooden floor and a ceiling of exposed wooden beams with whitewashed walls. The vast double bed had once been a four-poster, but to accommodate it under the low ceiling its canopy and the top of the posts had been sawn off and it was surrounded by rails from which hung mosquito netting, giving it a ghostly effect. The heavy wooden furniture, chest, wardrobe and chairs were dark with age, a modern note was a fitted basin with running water, but there was no colour in the room at all; the rugs were white sheepskin, the curtains dark brown. Téo looked round his depressing aspect with an enigmatical expression.

'The room in which the d'Argentières were born and died,' he murmured.

Madame overheard him and told him: 'The old Monsieur died in hospital, but as regards his predecessors I would not know.'

'And the other room?'

'In here, *monsieur*.'

She opened a connecting door. A couple of steps led down into a smaller apartment with a brass bedstead and light wood furniture. A crimson rug on the floor and white curtains made it look gay after the sombreness of the adjacent apartment. As in the other room, there was a basin and white towels.

'Thank you, *madame*, these rooms will do very nicely,' Téo announced, as the burly Georges knocked on the door to hand in their cases.

'Supper will be ready when you are, *monsieur*,' Madame Boulanger told them, 'and Monsieur d'Argentière always called me Annette.'

'You prefer that, *madame*?' Téo asked with a twinkle in his eye.

'It is as Monsieur pleases.'

'*Eh bien*, Monsieur does please,' Téo said gallantly—to Peta's annoyance; she thought he should be more formal with a servant, for that was all Madame Boulanger was, she told herself firmly, seeking reassurance.

A cry came from the passage outside and the handle of the door leading into the passage rattled.

'*Maman, Maman, on arrive?*'

The woman threw them an anxious look. 'My son,' she explained. She crossed to the further door, opened it and said sharply:

'Jean-Paul, *tu es méchant. Vas à ton lit.*'

155

Beyond her through the half open door Peta caught sight of a diminutive pyjama-clad figure.

'Introduce us, *madame*,' she said, smiling. 'I think he wants to meet us.'

Somewhat reluctantly, Annette opened the door wider to admit a boy of about seven years old, who came towards them eagerly. He was a sturdy well-grown child with a thatch of black hair. The eyes he raised to Téo's face were tawny gold.

'Are you my papa?' he asked.

'*Mon dieu!*' his mother exclaimed. '*Tu es bête!* You know you have no papa.' She turned to Téo. 'My husband was drowned at sea, but *le pauvre* will not accept that he cannot return.'

'Poor child,' Peta murmured softly, impulsively moving towards the boy, but it was Téo who attracted him, and she realised with a slight shock that their eyes were similar. Téo laid his hand on the black head.

'I will be a father to you,' he promised.

A gleam of satisfaction came into Annette's eyes, before she threw an apologetic glance towards Peta as if she feared this sudden adoption might be resented by her, and in fact Peta thought Téo was being rash. The boy would be about the same age that Marcel would have been had he lived, and she knew Téo still hungered for his son. Though she could not repulse any child, particularly a fatherless one, she would find it trying if he sought consolation with this one. He ought to have another son of his own.

Evidently Jean-Paul had been briefed about the new master's antecedents, for he asked excitedly:

'You will tell me all about Africa, *mon père*? Have you seen real live lions, elephants and ... and ... crocodiles?'

'Tomorrow, *mon enfant*,' Téo promised, stroking the rough black head. 'It is too late now, it's your bedtime and I have to have my supper. Go with Maman.'

156

Annette led her son away, and Peta said vehemently:

'Really, Téo, wasn't that a bit unnecessary? If he's going to call you father ... and did you notice, his eyes are like yours ... what will people think?'

'I don't care a damn what people think,' Téo returned. 'Drowned father my foot! That boy's a d'Argentière. The old man must have been virile right up into old age.'

Peta's eyes widened. 'Then you believe...?'

'It's obvious, isn't it? Annette Boulanger is a good-looking woman. It's only surprising Grandpère didn't leave him the estate.' His eyes became dreamy. 'Marcel would have been like him except that his eyes were like Lucie's.'

'Which goes to show the colour of his eyes proves nothing,' Peta pointed out. 'You said my eyes were like ... like Marcel's mother's, and we were no relation.'

'I said they reminded me of Marcel,' Téo corrected her. 'Lucie's eyes were hard as grey stones, and it wasn't only the colour, but the expression in them when you were scared. Marcel used to look at me like you did when he was frightened and wanted me to console him.'

Peta found cold comfort in being compared to a two-year-old toddler. Perhaps that was why Téo always called her *'mon enfant'*.

Yielding to a masochistic desire to turn the knife in her wound, she said:

'I couldn't be like your first wife, she was beautiful.'

'That is what drew me to her,' he told her. 'Young blood runs hot and isn't very discriminating. Lucie held me responsible for enticing her into a mode of life which she found intolerable, and my infatuation died in the face of her continual reproaches. My work was always between us.' He was staring moodily at the wall above her head as he made this revelation, the first time he had admitted that his first marriage had been a failure. Peta understood then how very reluctant he would be to effect another permanent union

157

and her heart sank. She had not got Lucie's beauty to aid her and he put no reliance upon what he believed was only a girlish fancy on her part. How could she ever convince him otherwise?

Téo withdrew his gaze from the wall and gave her a rueful smile.

'*Alors*, that's all past history now. What started it?'

'Jean-Paul.'

'Ah, *oui*. I must do something for that boy.'

'You seem adroit at contracting ambiguous relationships,' Peta said crossly. 'A wife who is no wife and a son whom you didn't beget.'

Téo refused to be ruffled. 'I could legally adopt him,' he said thoughtfully.

'Better find out a little more about him first,' Peta advised, 'and his handsome mother, who I think is a scheming hussy.'

Téo looked at her with laughter in his eyes.

'Jealous?'

'No, of course not, but I don't like seeing your generosity imposed upon.'

'That comes well from you,' he rebuked her, and she turned away with quivering lips. If he wanted to befriend Annette Boulanger and her fatherless brat she was in no position to criticise his wisdom, which was a very doubtful quantity in his dealings with herself. She had pinned all her hopes upon this period alone with him, and now it seemed her chances were to be jeopardised by his grandfather's mistress and his ... She began to laugh. The boy was Téo's uncle if he were in reality old d'Argentière's son.

'What's so funny?' Téo asked.

'Have you worked out what young Jean-Paul's relationship to you is, if your suppositions are correct?'

'Why, no ... *mon dieu!*' and he too laughed. The laughter cleared the air and he inquired:

'Which room would you like? This one or the funeral parlour next door?'

'This one every time, if you aren't scared of sleeping in that ghostly bed.'

'If I have a nightmare I'll call to you to come and drive the bogies away.' He peered at her intently. 'Would you come?'

'You're quite capable of dealing with any bogies that materialise,' she said disdainfully, for she was still sore over the intrusion of Jean-Paul and his mother. 'I wouldn't dream of intruding.'

Téo walked to the communicating door, took the key from the further side, locked it and laid the key on her dressing table.

'That wasn't necessary,' Peta told him, flushing.

He grinned. 'One never knows. I might walk in my sleep. Now you'll feel perfectly secure.'

She wanted to cry out that she had no need to feel secure, that if the inclination came to him to come through that door she would welcome him, but pride checked the words; instead she said dully:

'What will Madame Boulanger think?'

'What the devil does it matter what she thinks? Our matrimonial secrets are nothing to do with her. This sudden deference to public opinion is quite out of character, *mon enfant*, in one of your generation who make a point of flouting it. See you at supper.'

With which parting gibe he strolled out of the further door into the passage.

Annette served them a well cooked supper of chicken fricassée, *petits pois* and sauté potatoes, followed by sweet omelettes, cheese and fruit, saying she had had her own meal, when Téo invited her to join them. Jean-Paul, she told them, was asleep and Monsieur had been very kind to humour him, but he mustn't let him become a nuisance.

'He could never be that,' Téo declared.

Annette smiled sagely. Monsieur had not had much experience of small boys and their tiresome ways, but doubtless the time would come when he would learn. She looked archly at Peta, who, recalling the locked door, was unreceptive. She waited upon them looking the picture of demure respectability, but the glances she threw towards Téo were anything but demure as she batted her long eyelashes. Peta noticed them and presently saw with dismay that Téo was returning them.

Annette brought coffee to them in the *salon*, as she called it, a room the old master had rarely used, but she had cleaned it and opened it up for their arrival. It was simply furnished with carved wooden high-backed settles and chairs and a refectory table. A few watercolours of cattle and horses amid the marshes adorned the walls.

'Done for the tourists,' Annette told them. 'There are many here in the summer, including artists. We had one staying here for a while, until Monsieur quarrelled with him. He left the pictures to pay his rent.'

A small fire of logs burned in the huge grate, for the evening was chill, and gave a cheerful note to the long low room. Peta drew up a stool in front of it; she felt the cold after Africa.

Téo bade Annette to sit down and take coffee with them, an invitation she had evidently expected, for she had brought three cups.

'Madame will wish to take over the running of the house?' she inquired, eyeing Peta doubtfully. She spoke with a strong Provençal accent so that the girl found her French difficult to follow. 'I will give to you the keys of the storerooms.'

'Oh no,' Peta exclaimed quickly. 'I've no idea of how such a place is run. I'll be glad if you will continue as long as you're here.'

'As Madame wishes,' Annette murmured, dropping her eyelids to conceal the satisfaction in their dark depths.

'But you will no doubt instruct her?' Téo suggested, looking displeased. 'She should learn how to manage the household.'

'With pleasure, *monsieur*.'

Peta was about to protest that there was no point in imbibing a lot of useless instructions when she would soon be leaving, but Annette did not know that, so she said nothing. She was fairly certain that if she left Madame Boulanger would stay on indefinitely. She ought to be glad that Téo would have the services of an efficient housekeeper, but that was beyond her, for she was becoming wildly jealous. Her husband, and he was her husband for the time being, was getting on far too well with this handsome woman. He was questioning her eagerly about the estate and the staff, to Peta's exclusion, so that finally she said she was tired and would go to bed. Annette's dark eyes followed her exit speculatively; she had not missed the significance of the two rooms.

Peta entered her bedroom in a mood of revolt. She was not going to allow Annette Boulanger to usurp her rights without a fight! The wine she had drunk at supper had warmed her blood and blurred reasonable thought. Wine loosens inhibitions and hers were swept away tonight. She had been stung by Annette's amorous glances that Téo had not repelled, though it was possible he had not appreciated their meaning, and Annette held a trump card with the boy, who was the same age as Marcel would have been. She could halt the woman's machinations if she was brave enough, and at that moment she had courage for any action that would enable her to hold her own.

From her cases—she had not finished unpacking, there had not been time before supper—she took out the nightgown and negligée that her mother had chosen for her wedding night. At the time of the purchase she had scorned the flimsy garments, for she would never wear them and regretted her mother's extravagance. Now she put them on. The delicate silk lining and nylon over-slip clung to her long limbs, which surely had become more rounded of late. The colour was pale apricot which toned with her tanned skin and emphasised the dense blackness of her hair that was so much finer in texture than Annette's wiry locks. But colour was immaterial for an encounter in the dark. Excitement brought a vivid flush to her cheeks and caused her eyes to shine like stars. She put scent behind her ears and on her wrists. Perdita Cartwright, the virginal young Amazon, was about to play the seductress and she meant to use every art to attain her end. This was her wedding night, and she did not mean to spend it alone.

Satisfied that she could do no more to enhance her appearance, she listened for sounds from behind the locked door. There were none; Téo had not yet come upstairs. When he did he would find her in his bed. Peta smiled triumphantly as she imagined his surprise and her heart quickened at the thought of his embrace, for surely he could not deny her when she was actually there awaiting him. Annette had been giving him cognac with his coffee which would have warmed him, and as far as she knew he had been celibate for some time. She should be able to sweep away his resistance. She was not doing anything wrong, she was his wife and had every right to claim him, and she would convince him at last that her love was an adult emotion and not a schoolgirl's crush.

She went to pick up the key.

It was cold and heavy in her hand and its chill seemed to strike up her arm and into her heart, bringing a return of sanity. If Téo took her tonight there could be no annulment, and he did not wish for a permanent tie. To seek to betray him through his senses was a mean trick to play

162

after all his kindness to her. Either he would repulse her, which would hurt her pride unbearably, or he would yield and regret his action ever after. Either way she would be no nearer to her heart's desire, which was to win his lasting love, and she might antagonise him beyond all hope of reconciliation.

She let the key drop back on the table and turned towards her bed. Never had she felt more lonely or more unwanted, and it was her wedding night.

Peta was awakened by a banging on her door and opening her bleary eyes—she had cried herself to sleep—she saw that sunshine was pouring in through the thin curtains.

'*Entrez*,' she murmured.

The handle turned and Jean-Paul came bounding into the room fully dressed and beaming.

'*Bonjour, madame*,' he carolled, 'and it is a *bon* day. *Mon papa* and I are about to ride, and he asks that you will join us.'

Annette appeared bearing a tray of coffee and proceeded to scold her son for intruding.

'It's all right,' Peta intervened as the child shrank from his mother's angry voice. 'He hasn't disturbed me and it's quite time I woke up. No ... please let him stay,' as Annette harshly bade the boy be gone.

'He makes himself a nuisance,' his mother grumbled, then with a change of tone. 'The horses will be at the door in half an hour and *déjeuner* will be ready upon your return. You sleep well, *n'est-ce pas*?' She looked curiously at the tumbled bed and, guessing what was in her mind, Peta blushed.

'Very well, thank you,' she said primly. 'I'll be down in half an hour.'

Jean-Paul was hopping about on one leg.

'*Depêchez-vous, madame*,' he urged.

163

'Control your impatience,' Annette snapped. 'Madame has the garments for the ride?'

Téo had insisted that Peta bought jodhpurs and boots in anticipation of much riding so she was able to say she had indeed got the right garments.

The hot coffee revived her and after she had washed and dressed in the riding clothes which suited her slender height so well her spirits rose. The painful thoughts of the previous evening evaporated like an evil mist before the bright sunshine. She was young, in love and not without hope. Except for her sharpness towards her son, Annette had been friendly, Jean-Paul even more so, and her dark forebodings seemed without ground.

Téo was waiting for her when she came down looking spruce and elegant in breeches, boots and a yellow sweater. From somewhere he had acquired one of the large felt hats the herdsmen wore which he had put on at a rakish angle so that it gave him a devil-may-care air. Jean-Paul was already mounted on his pony, which he sat like a centaur. For Peta and Téo there were two white horses of the sturdy Camargue breed, not very big animals but strong and wiry. A *gardien* hovered at a respectful distance who had been detailed to show them around. He was a typical cowhand, lean and weatherbeaten, and carried the three-pronged spear that was used to control the cattle.

Peta swung herself unaided into her saddle; she loved riding and it was a long time since she had had an opportunity to do any. Téo looked up at her with an approving grin.

'Your mount is not quite like Mustapha, but he's a good beast,' he said. 'These horses are up to any weight and I know that you can ride well.'

She was ridiculously pleased that he remembered that incident, which was when it had all begun. He mounted his own animal and they trotted away to inspect his new

164

domain, the *gardien* following. Presently Téo checked and beckoned to him to come up alongside and forthwith they plunged into an animated conversation. The horses splashed through shallow meres and cantered on higher ground, while Jean-Paul supplied Peta with any information she needed. The horses, he told her, knew by instinct whether the ground was safe. Oh yes, there were some quagmires in places which were quite unpleasant.

The breeding of black cattle and white horses was traditional, and the remaining ranches continued with it as a point of honour. He did not put it quite so lucidly, as he lacked the vocabulary, but Peta understood what he meant. When he grew up he intended to be a *gardien*, one of the proud fraternity of herdsmen who dedicated themselves to preserving the Camargue.

'People come from ever so far away to photograph them,' he told her. Then abruptly he asked: 'Were you with *mon père* in Maroc?'

Peta checked a desire to correct him. Téo was not his father and she disliked hearing him call him so, but it was not her business. Téo intended to adopt this engaging youngster, might even in the course of time marry Annette when he was free, that was if he could marry his step-grandmother; she was hazy about French law upon that point. It would be an ideal arrangement from the boy's point of view, since Annette possessed all the competency she lacked herself and he would not look for love. Annette would not come between him and his work as Lucie had done, she would share it.

Jean-Paul had evidently been puzzling over their relationships, and had worked it out to his satisfaction, for after her admission that she had lived with Téo in Morocco, he said:

'In Africa a man can have lots of wives, *n'est-ce pas*, and Papa married you when he went there. My *maman* had to

165

stay behind to look after *le grand monsieur* and me.'

Peta was unbearably stung by this naïve explanation. If Téo adopted Jean-Paul the boy would naturally call him Papa, but he had not done so yet, and the child's assumption that he was his natural father was infinitely galling with its implications with regard to Annette. Téo had not thought of the complications when he had so blithely said he would be a father to the boy, who had taken him literally. She dared not try to put him right, but she would tell Téo he must somehow make the situation clear to him. Then depression swept over her again. Did it matter very much what the child thought, or anyone else for that matter? She would not be staying long, for after a few weeks Téo would remind her it was time the bond between them was severed, the first step towards which would be her departure. The green landscape swam before her eyes in a mist of tears.

Her expression was not missed by the observant child.

'*Madame*, you are *triste*!' he exclaimed. 'Is it that you want your *déjeuner* or do you weep for Maroc?'

Peta dashed her hand across her eyes and managed a shaky laugh.

'Neither, a fly got in my eye. See, Monsieur is far ahead, let's gallop to catch up with him.'

She urged her mount forward and the swift exercise did much to restore her spirits, so that by the time they returned she was able to laugh and chatter with the boy.

In the days that followed, Téo became submerged in the business of the estate and he seemed to forget that Peta was not a permanency. She suspected that in his preoccupation with other matters he had shelved her problems, even forgotten that they existed. She was content that it should be so, for she had no wish to leave, she enjoyed ranch life and was grateful for the casual friendliness Téo extended to her. He classed her with Jean-Paul, she thought wryly; they were two children to be indulged and spoiled but firmly checked if they showed signs of becoming rebellious. Not that she ever did—she had no cause to quarrel with her present existence, except for the ever-present frustration of being so near to her husband and yet separated from him by his indifference.

But below the surface tranquillity of their lives were undercurrents. It was not long before Peta realised that Annette had little love for her son. Perhaps his advent had been so great an embarrassment to her it had drowned her softer feelings, for few people believed the polite fiction of a father lost at sea and the country folk had not hesitated to smirch her name. Since her son had failed to inherit the Mas from his real parent, she vented her disappointment upon his innocent head. In Téo's presence she was all maternal solicitude, but Peta often heard her scolding Jean-Paul and she was not above slapping him when his high spirits irritated her.

Consequently Jean-Paul attached himself to Téo with touching devotion, following him everywhere like a little dog, being followed in his turn by Di-di, a mongrel whelp he had befriended. Téo was never impatient with him, and however busy he was would never send him away, except when it was bedtime. He discovered that the child was not being schooled, and in explanation Annette told him that her son did not get on with the local children. They had teased him so mercilessly that she had been forced to keep him at home. The old master had promised to send him to a boarding school, but ... She shrugged her shoulders and looked at Téo appealingly.

'I myself cannot afford the fees, and it will be as bad for him there unless Monsieur really means to adopt him.'

'Poor little boy!' Téo exclaimed, visualising the un-enviable position of the fatherless waif. 'He shan't go to school again until he has a right to his name.'

Meanwhile Jean-Paul ought to have lessons and he suggested that Peta might be able to undertake them.

'You were training to be some sort of teacher, weren't you?' he asked.

'For physical training, and it's a long way from that to the three R's,' she said, smiling. 'However, if there's no alternative, I'll try what I can do for him.'

'You can manage the basic, I'm sure,' he told her. 'And I'll help when I've time. Perdita, I love that boy.'

He made the admission as if he were ashamed of it, and Peta stifled a sigh. Had love become so alien to him that he feared to confess it? His whole face softened when he spoke of Jean-Paul as it had never softened for her. But she was not so petty as to be jealous of a child, and she said gently:

'He's very lovable, and I don't think his mother gives him much affection.'

The momentary softness left Téo's face and he said coldly:

'She seems to me to be a most exemplary parent, but she is very busy and children do need a measure of discipline. She finds him a handful at times, for he has reached an age when he should have a man's control, but she does her best for him. She is a most efficient woman and I don't know what we would have done without her.'

This praise of Madame Boulanger with its covert thrust at her own uselessness was bitter gall to Peta. With Annette running the domestic side of the Mas she had no occupation, and she was being denied children of her own.

With her voice shaking she said: 'What a pity you became involved with me. If you hadn't you could have become Jean-Paul's stepfather and secured Madame Boulanger's services for all time.'

His brows drew together in a frown.

'Don't be childish,' he bade her severely.

'I was only stating the obvious. Oh, all right,' as she saw his lips framing a biting retort, 'I'll teach this little byblow

168

to please you, which is something apparently Annette can't do.'

'Never call him that,' Téo cried fiercely. 'Soon he'll bear my name, and he's as much right here as I have.'

'And more than I have, though I also bear your name—temporarily.'

'What do you mean by that?'

'This ... er ... arrangement was never intended to be permanent, was it?' She veiled her eyes with her long lashes to conceal the eagerness with which she waited for his reply.

When it came it was not what she hoped for.

'You're tired of the Mas?' he asked anxiously. 'You're bored here? I was afraid you might be.'

'Not at all, but I have my own life to lead. There's no future for me here.'

She looked at him wistfully, but he had turned to stare out of the window and missed the yearning in her eyes.

'I see your point,' he told her, 'and it's only to be expected.' (What did he mean by that?) 'However, I would be grateful if you would stay here until the spring. By then everything should be running smoothly.'

'Of course I will,' she promised. 'I ... I'll be glad to be useful.'

'More than that, *ma mie*.'

She felt her heart lift with gladness, but he douched her elation immediately by adding: 'It's a pity you're not more interested in housekeeping, but I couldn't expect domesticity from a prospective Olympic champion, and Jean-Paul won't need you when he goes to school.'

So it was only as a governess that he wanted her to stay; nonetheless the spring was some months away and much might happen before it came.

Jean-Paul was a bright boy and seemed to be eager to learn. Téo formed the habit of taking him out for a ride before he settled to his books on the principle that as with a frisky horse he could 'get the tickle out of his feet', before setting to work. Peta sometimes accompanied them, but more often not, as she sensed Téo liked to have the child to himself. Annette accepted their arrangements, though Peta was aware that she resented them, but she did not dare to oppose Téo.

Came a morning when Jean-Paul was late back from his outing. It was a dank misty day and Peta was in the dining room arranging his books for his lesson. The carpet had arrived from Rabat and was a bright note in the plain room. It did not cover all the floor and there was an expanse of polished wood surrounding it which had just been cleaned.

Jean-Paul came straight into the room wearing his muddy jeans and boots, followed by the whelp he had adopted, a shaggy coated dog with big paws. These were wet and were pattering the shining wood, while the boy sprinkled mud on the carpet.

'I'm sorry I'm late, *madame*,' he said, 'but I thought I'd better let you know I'm back before I went to change.'

'That's all right, Jean-Paul,' Peta told him, admiring the brilliant colour in his cheeks from the cold ride. 'There's no hurry. Run along and clean up.'

A tornado descended upon them through the open door. Perhaps Annette had some excuse for her fury, for she had done the room early that morning and boy and dog were ruining her efforts, but there was no excuse for her subsequent actions.

'Jean-Paul,' she shrilled, 'what do you mean by coming in here in that state and bringing that disgusting animal in doors? Look at the mess you've made! Get out at once— and you too!' She aimed a kick at the dog. She did not actually touch it, but her intention was plain and the beast gave a yelp and slunk under the table.

'You mustn't kick my dog!' Jean-Paul cried. 'Di-di, Di-

170

di, come here. Did she hurt you?' He crawled under the table after the animal.

'I'll get Georges to shoot that mangy brute,' Annette stormed. 'Then you can't bring him inside again, while as for you, you know what you're in for, my boy!'

Jean-Paul glared up at her from his refuge under the table, his arms about the dog.

'I'll tell my *papa* about you. He won't let Georges touch Di-di.'

'We'll see about that!' She made an ineffective attempt to reach her son.

'Please, Annette,' Peta intervened, 'he only came in to apologise for being late and I'm sure he didn't mean to make a mess. I'll clean it up when he's gone to change.'

Annette straightened herself too deeply incensed to listen to reason. Her black eyes glittered with malice as she turned upon Peta.

'*Tiens,* that would be a change! You never soil your hands if you can avoid it, do you, *madame?* You're too dainty even to warm the master's bed, the door between you is locked, *n'est-ce pas?* Fortunately for him I am not so cold. I know what men need. Why do you linger here? Nobody wants you, and once you've gone I can take my rightful place. The master has promised that I shall, and I understand him, which you could never do. In the meantime I will not have you spoiling my son. You're teaching him to disobey me.' She turned to the door and shouted down the passage, 'Georges!'

Peta turned cold. Téo had told this virulent woman the true position and she had implied that he had already taken her to share his bed. She recalled Zillah, to whom physically Annette bore a slight resemblance; she was his type, he liked his women ripe and opulent, and he had been unable to resist her advances. Moreover, he had praised her competence. What chance had Peta against such a rival? The dice

171

had been loaded against her from the start.

Georges came limping through the door; an old man who had injured his leg in a riding accident, he did all the rough work for Annette, fetching in fuel and cleaning the grates. He looked upon her as the mistress of the Mas.

'Take that dog out and shoot it,' Annette commanded.

Jean-Paul sprang out from under the table and hurled himself upon his mother, pummelling her with his fists.

'*Non, non!*' he shrieked. 'You cannot, you shall not!'

Annette seized his wrists. 'For this you will spend the rest of the day in the cellar!'

Di-di, frightened by the uproar, rushed round the room pursued by Georges and finally collapsed at Peta's feet, looking up at her with imploring brown eyes.

'No, Georges,' she said as the man approached her. 'Leave him with me.'

The man paused uncertainly, glancing at Annette, who smiled grimly.

'Later,' she said significantly to her henchman. She took hold of the back of Jean-Paul's jersey collar and dragged him towards the door. 'The cellar may cool your temper, *mon garçon.*'

Jean-Paul shrieked anew. '*Non*, Maman, *non!* It is dark and cold and I will be frightened!'

'Madame Boulanger——' Peta began to protest.

'Keep out of this,' Annette snapped. 'He's my child.'

At that moment Téo walked into the room. Instantly Jean-Paul twisted free from his mother's hold and fled to him, clinging to his jacket sobbing hysterically. Téo looked round the room, noting the shivering dog, Georges' sheepish look, Annette's angry frown and Peta's white face as she surveyed him with wide accusing eyes.

'*Mon dieu*, what happens here?' he demanded.

They all started to speak at once and he held up his hand.

172

'*Taisez-vous!* Perdita, please to explain.'

Before she could open her mouth, Jean-Paul cried;

'Maman sent for Georges to take Di-di and shoot him and she is going to lock me in the cellar. Papa, don't let her, please, please!'

'Jean-Paul mistakes . . .' Annette began.

'*Un moment, madame,*' Téo stopped her coldly. 'Georges, you may go, but unless you want to be instantly dismissed you will never, I repeat, never harm the boy's dog. Is that understood?'

'*Oui, monsieur.*' The man touched his forelock and stumped out of the room. Téo sat down and took Jean-Paul on to his knees, his eyes fixed sternly upon Annette.

'Now, *madame*, is it a practice of yours to shut this little one in the cellar when he annoys you?'

'The child must be punished when he is disobedient,' Annette returned calmly. 'The cellar subdues him.'

'Barbarous,' Téo told her succinctly. 'Never do it again. I will correct Jean-Paul when necessary. What was his fault upon this occasion?'

Annette quivered with outrage as she indicated the floor, which had not been improved by Georges' boots and the ensuing fracas.

'He brings mud in here, also his filthy dog, and when I protest he is rude.'

'He came in to apologise for being late,' Peta interposed. 'He didn't realise he was making a mess of the floor, but what's a little mud? It'll brush off.'

Annette shot her a glance of pure hate.

'So you think, *madame*, but someone has to do the brushing.' She turned to Téo, her manner becoming ingratiating. 'Perhaps I was too hasty, *monsieur*, but I disliked so much to see your so beautiful carpet from Maroc marred. As for the dog, it should not be allowed in the house, it is not sanitary.'

173

'Maybe, but I would put up with worse things to save this little one so much distress,' Téo informed her stroking Jean-Paul's head. '*Eh bien*, this would seem to be a storm in a teacup, but ...' his face grew stern ... 'it might be as well, Madame Boulanger, if you accelerated your plans for the dress shop in Arles and recalled to mind that the extra funds you require to start it depend upon my good will.'

Both Peta and Annette stared at him dumbfounded, Peta because this was the first she had heard of such a scheme and Annette because she had imagined that Téo could not do without her. The Provençale recovered first.

'But, *monsieur*,' she objected, 'it was a thought for the future. There is no haste ...'

'I think there is,' Téo interrupted. 'I see no reason for delay.'

'*Mais ... mais* ... how can you manage if I go? Madame is not *au fait* with the running of the Mas, and she will not be staying ...'

Téo glanced at Peta. 'That's our business, but she would never leave me in the lurch.'

'Neither will I,' Annette declared stoutly. She moved nearer to Téo, her lips curved in a sensuous smile. 'Monsieur Théodore,' she went on softly, 'all this is a mere *bagatelle*. The dog is in no danger from me and Jean-Paul shall be spared the cellar if that is your wish, but I cannot leave you, nor can you really desire to dispense with me. I serve you too well ... in so many different ways.'

The exultation that had begun to rise in Peta at Annette's dismissal faded away. The woman's insinuation was obvious. Even if she did go and Téo turned to her nothing could wipe out the insult he had offered to her by giving to his housekeeper all that he withheld from herself. She was his wife, even if only in name, and surely he owed her a semblance of fidelity under his own roof.

Téo put Jean-Paul from off his knee and rose to his feet.

'Enough,' he said shortly. 'Jean-Paul, you had better go and clean up. Madame Boulanger...' his use of her surname indicated that she was not forgiven '...I'm sure your duties call you as do mine. We will speak again when I have more leisure.'

'But Di-di?' Jean-Paul asked anxiously, not certain that his pet was safe.

Téo smiled. 'If you wish him to become a house dog he must have a bath. Perhaps *madame ma femme* will help you to give him one instead of today's lessons, for which I'm sure you're too disturbed. Will you, Perdita?'

He looked at her with a mingling of rueful appeal and apology in his glance, but Peta met his eyes with a stony stare. His expression indicated remorse for past guilt, but she was not going to allow him to placate her, her hurt was too great.

'That's a very good idea,' she agreed. 'Run along, Jean-Paul, I will keep Di-di until you return and then we'll attend to his toilet.'

Annette uttered an exclamation of disgust and flounced out of the room. Téo took a step towards his wife.

'Perdita?'

'Quite a dramatic scene,' she said coolly, ignoring the query in his voice and the soft light in his tawny eyes. She knew she was weak where he was concerned, but this time she did not intend to relent. 'It was a good thing you came in when you did, but there's no need for you to stay any longer. I know you're always busy.'

The light died out of his face and he drew back.

'I want to talk to you after supper,' he said with equal frostiness. 'It is necessary to rearrange the *ménage* here.'

'I shall be available.'

He seemed about to say more, then changed his mind and went out of the room. Peta absently stroked Di-di's rough coat. The *ménage* certainly did need rearranging, and after supper she would tell him she had decided to leave at once.

# CHAPTER TEN

PETA dressed with care for what she determined would be her last supper at the Mas. She had some money left from her father's cheque and she would stay at a hotel in Marseilles until she had procured her separate passport. Téo would probably offer to supplement it, but she was resolved to take nothing from him. She could always wire to her father for additional funds if she were in difficulties.

Jean-Paul was sound asleep with Di-di beside him. He had begged for the dog's company, being fearful that Annette would find a way to dispose of him in the night. As the animal was clean and combed after his bath, Peta had sanctioned his presence and had informed Annette that she had done so. Madame Boulanger had given her a sour smile and said deprecatingly:

'I must bow to Madame's wishes *as long as she is here.*'

Peta had felt a slight qualm at this ambiguity, but Jean-Paul would have Téo's protection for himself and his dog, and the master had very definitely said he would extend it to them.

During the afternoon one of their neighbours' sons had rung up to invite himself for the evening. He had come down from Paris on a flying visit and was anxious to meet the new owner of Mas d'Argentière. Téo had extended a cordial invitation to Emile Dupont and Peta suspected he felt as she did that a stranger's presence would relieve any tension between them at supper, for Annette took that meal with them now.

She put on one of her trousseau dresses that her mother had chosen and Téo had not seen. It was of red silk with a square neck and full chiffon sleeves. At the time of purchase she had thought it was too dressy, but now she was glad of its style; it would give her confidence. About her throat she fastened the silver necklace Téo had bought for her in Morocco. Her black hair, growing long now, shone like a blackbird's wing, the ends curling attractively below her ears. She rarely used make-up, but tonight she enhanced her eyes with painted shadow and was pleased to see how it made them look very big and mysterious, their natural grey turning almost to violet. It would be difficult now to identify her with the shabby urchin whom Téo had rescued in Casablanca, she thought with satisfaction. Love had matured her and she had become a woman fully fledged.

Emile was a slim young man with long hair and a moustache, wearing an exotic velvet jacket. He was, he told them, a poet and rarely visited his home in the Camargue, but he had come in search of inspiration for a threnody he was writing, and he thought the melancholy of the flat lands and wide skies would put him in the right mood. Téo looked a little taken aback by this expansiveness and Peta had to stifle a giggle. Both Monsieur Dupont's appearance and his speech were flamboyant.

'Had I known we had such a beautiful neighbour I would have come sooner,' he declared as he kissed her fingertips. 'You possess the poetry of motion, *madame*, I shall write an ode to you as Atalanta, the fleet of foot.'

'You're not so far out, *mon vieux*,' Téo said, laughing. 'My wife is an athlete.'

Emile closed his eyes and shuddered. '*Non, non,* not that word, which conjures up visions of brawny muscles. Rather is Madame the spirit of the wind, a creature of air and fire.'

Peta thought he was talking nonsense, but he seemed to amuse Téo, whose eyes were sparkling mischievously, but she thought his admiration was genuine and that pleased her; it would do Téo good to find that she could attract other men, and from the way he kept looking at her he seemed to be viewing her with new eyes.

'You're not the sort of person I'd expect to come out of a Camargue ranch,' Téo said to his guest as they went into supper.

'Poets are born in unlikely places,' Emile returned. 'The divine fire falls indiscriminatingly, and old Provence was famed for its troubadours. But I do not know why I was singled out, for my relatives are all barbarians who think only of cows and my spiritual home is Paris.'

Annette joined them at the supper table, demurely dressed in black with a white lace fichu. She eyed Emile with barely concealed contempt. To her bucolic mind such creatures were not men at all. But he proved good company during the meal, describing his friends and colleagues with wit and malicious humour, and Peta was grateful for the diversion from her sad thoughts. Téo was looking particularly distinguished tonight, wearing a black jacket and a white silk shirt, his smooth brown head a contrast to their guest's flowing locks. Peta hardly dared to look at him lest her resolution should waver, and she gave all her attention to the poet. Annette was subdued and her eyes kept seeking Téo's with a conciliatory expression. Evidently she feared she had offended him. But they'll soon make it up when I've gone, Peta thought despondently, and hoped that once the woman had obtained what she wanted she would be kinder to Jean-Paul.

Emile left early after coffee and cognac, for the wind was rising and he did not want to be caught in the mistral's chilly blast.

'But I shall come again soon,' he said to Peta. 'You are my muse. I shall wish to read to you my poem about Atalanta.'

'I'm honoured,' she murmured, keeping her eyes down-cast lest he should glimpse her merriment.

But when Emile came again she would be gone.

Annette removed the used whisky glasses and the coffee cups and when she had left, Téo locked the door of the salon.

'So we shall not be interrupted,' he told Peta. 'I believe you wished to talk to me, and I've a proposition I want to put to you.'

He came back into the middle of the room and stared down at her where she sat beside the fire, the burning logs casting a roseate glow over the long folds of red silk that fell to her feet, her hands clasped about her crossed knee.

'That's a very attractive dress,' he remarked, 'and young Emile seemed much impressed by you.'

She laughed. 'Terrible poseur, wasn't he? I don't think he'd have been impressed if he'd seen me in my d'jellaba ...' She stopped, confused. Why had she mentioned that historic garment? The last thing she wanted to do was to recall their days of comradeship together. Turning her gaze to the fire, she said quietly:

'I've decided I want to go home, and I'd like to leave tomorrow.'

Téo turned to the drinks table on which the cognac and clean glasses still reposed and poured himself a stiff tot. His face was expressionless. 'You promised to stay until the spring,' he reminded her.

'I know I did, but that was before I knew ... everything.'

'Everything? I was not aware that I had concealed any-thing from you.'

'No, it's obvious. There's no need to go into details.' She kept her gaze on the fire. 'My mind is made up. It's time I left.'

Téo sat down opposite to her on the other side of the hearth.

'I disagree with you,' he said pleasantly. 'We will go into all the details. First and foremost, is it the life here that is too monotonous for you? You said the other day it was not, but you may have been trying to spare my feelings.'

'No, Téo, it's not that at all,' she told him. 'I love the Mas, and I shall always be glad that I've stayed here, but as I said then, I've my own life to lead and it's time I took it up where I left off.'

'Is your athletic career so much to you?'

He seemed to be deliberately obtuse, or did he think she would not mind about Annette? As she did not answer, he went on:

'Actually I belive you've forgotten all about it.' He paused, looking at her searchingly, but she gave no response, and he went on:

'Perhaps you've heard from the boy-friend in Maroc? Do you wish to join him?'

'I haven't heard from Keith and I don't care if I never do,' Peta returned. She turned her head to face him. 'It's for none of those reasons that I'm going. Since you want the truth, I find my position here intolerable. Can't you understand how Annette humiliates me?'

'If she has dared to be insolent——' he began, and Peta raised her hand to check him.

'You know she hasn't, but you've told her ours isn't a real marriage.'

'I have not, but she may have deduced it.'

'Then you must have given her reason for the deduction, and I can't—I cannot—live under the same roof as my husband's mistress.'

'If she's told you she is she lied,' Téo said emphatically.

Peta shook her head mournfully. 'Be honest with me, Téo, I can take it. You're giving her money?'

He sprang to his feet and began to pace the room.

'Annette has plans for a shop in Arles. I agreed to finance

her if she would let me adopt Jean-Paul. I was going to ask you if you felt equal to taking over from her, as I think the sooner she is out of the house the better for us all. She's a disruptive influence.'

'You mean you've already grown tired of her?' Peta inquired. 'It's a usual procedure, isn't it, to set the ex-mistress up in business, but I'm not interested in taking her leavings.'

'My grandfather's ex-mistress,' Téo corrected her. He came to a halt in front of her with a gleam in his eyes. Peta sensed excitement in him and wondered if it were her departure that was arousing it. Once free of her he could live openly with Annette, who could quite well run her business in Arles from the Mas.

'It's immaterial,' Peta said wearily. 'Do what you like, for I shall be far away.'

'I think not.' His tone was jubilant and she looked up at him with surprise. 'What it boils down to is that you want to run away from me and Jean-Paul who both need you and the Mas which you say you love, merely out of jealousy of Annette Boulanger.'

'Téo!' She sprang to her feet, her face flushed with indignation. 'And if I am jealous, who could blame me? You extol her virtues, you sleep with her . . .'

'*Tais-toi!*' he interrupted, and pulled her into his arms. Peta went limp; she had no resistance against physical contact with him. All other emotions were swept away in a great wave of love and longing. Her arms crept round his neck as he bent his head to hers and their lips met in a long kiss that seemed to draw her very soul from her body. He held her fiercely, possessively against his hard lean chest and her limbs seemed to melt against him.

Someone knocked on the door, but they took no notice and presently the intruder went away.

At length Téo released her with a long sigh.

'Now do you want to leave me?'

She sank down trembling on her former seat.

'If only you loved me!'

'But, *chérie*, of course I love you. From the first moment I saw you I was aware of some affinity between us, although I believed you were a boy. You looked so gallant and intrepid on that great horse, and you looked at me with eyes like Marcel's. That is why I got you out of Casa, I couldn't let you rot in a Moorish prison. Later when I discovered you were a girl, I began to fall in love with you.' He looked almost ashamed to confess it. 'I knew it was ridiculous. I should have had more sense at my age.'

'But when we were in the ruined kasbah and I told you how I felt you repulsed me, calling me a child and my love a silly infatuation.'

'That was the difficulty. You were such a child and it would not have been fair to take advantage of your youth and inexperience. You saw me as a romantic figure who had rescued you, whereas I'm only an ordinary middle-aged widower. I was sure that your fancy for me would soon fade when you returned to normal life.'

Peta looked at him reproachfully. Nicely groomed in his well-fitting evening clothes he appeared anything but ordinary, and his maturity had always attracted her; it set him apart from the gauche youths who had been her associates.

'You hurt me very much, Téo, with your indifference, which you now say was a pretence, and though you decry yourself, I haven't met anyone who can compare with you.'

'Nice of you to say so, and if I misjudged you, remember that I had made one bad mistake and dared not risk another. Lucie swore she loved me, but her infatuation soon died before the harsh reality of the life she had to lead with me. She wanted a divorce and to take Marcel away from me.'

Peta moved restlessly. 'Will she always come between

183

us?' she asked sadly.

'She never did. I'm only explaining why I didn't declare myself. I nearly did more than once, and when I asked you to marry me, and it seemed I was wise, for when you were ill you called incessantly for that boy-friend of yours.'

'I wasn't aware I did so. I think I confused him with you.'

'*Alors*, it led me to believe there was more between you than you had admitted, and after all, he was nearer your age than I was. When I contacted him over the phone he sounded a pleasant youth, though not exactly ardent. I quite expected him to turn up again in your life, so I did not want to bind you to me irrevocably. If I contained myself, the marriage could be dissolved whenever you wished, but I insisted upon your visit here. There was a faint chance you might turn to me, but if you found you loathed the place then I would have to let you go, but you say you like it.'

'I would be content to spend the rest of my life here,' Peta assured him earnestly, 'so long as you are with me.'

She stretched out her arms to him and he came and knelt beside her, encircling her waist with his.

'And the Olympic championship?' he asked softly.

'A young girl's dream. I forgot it months ago. But what has convinced you that I do care?'

His eyes glinted with mischief. 'Your jealousy of Annette.'

'Oh, really, Téo, I could be merely jealous of my usurped prerogatives, but it's not that,' she added hastily as he looked up at her doubtfully. 'I do love you, I always shall, and I'm grown up now.'

'I believe you are.' He tried to draw her closer, but she put her hand against his chest to hold him off.

'Have you slept with Annette?'

'Most certainly not, what do you think I am?' he demanded indignantly. 'The woman had her uses, but that was not one of them, and I'll be glad to be rid of her. She bullies poor little Jean-Paul and he'll be a different child when she's gone.' He looked suddenly anxious. 'You're not jealous of *him*?'

'No, Téo, and once he's free of his mother he'll be all ours, and I hope...' Peta stopped and blushed.

'You hope—what?' Téo murmured, gathering her close in the circle of his arms, his lips against her ear, and this time she did not resist.

'I'll be able to give him a brother and perhaps a sister.'

'You can't do that without my help,' Téo pointed out, 'but that will be forthcoming. No more locked doors, *chérie*.'

She told him how she had nearly gone to him on their wedding night.

'You don't know how hard I found it not to come to you,' he told her ruefully. 'That is why I gave you the key. I had to be sure you could live my life.'

The knocking at the *salon* door was repeated, this time more loudly.

'Hadn't you better go and see if anything is wrong?' Peta asked.

'I suppose so, though I expect it's only Annette,' Téo replied. 'She's thought up an excuse to interrupt us.' He rose reluctantly and went to open it.

It was Annette, wearing a quilted dressing gown, her magnificent hair in two long braids.

'*Pardon, monsieur*,' she said, 'but I cannot sleep with that dog that Madame insisted should repose with Jean-Paul.' She threw Peta a venomous glance. 'His room opens into mine and the brute scratches and growls. The mistral must have unsettled him.'

Téo laughed heartlessly. 'More likely it is your proximity, *madame*. You can't fool a dog. He knows you meant

185

to have him executed. *Alors*, we will soon remedy that. With your permission, Jean-Paul shall change his lodgings. The guest room will be vacant tonight.'

Annette knew then that her hopes were dashed. She said with dignity, 'As Monsieur pleases. If he does not mind a disturbed night, who am I to object?'

So Jean-Paul slept in Peta's bed with the dog at his feet, and Peta occupied the great fourposter. Outside the mistral howled, lashing the cypress trees, but Peta, close in Téo's arms, heard its shrieks without apprehension. Camargue storms could not alarm her, for she had found safe haven.

# Now available!

# COLLECTION EDITIONS

## of Classic Romances

Harlequin proudly presents a nostalgic collection of the best-selling romance novels of former years. This is a rare series of 100 books, lovingly reissued in beautifully designed new covers. And the cost is only 75¢ each. See complete listing on accompanying pages.

## *Not sold in stores.*

# Harlequin Collection Editions

*Please note: The number in brackets indicates the
original Harlequin Romance number.*

# Harlequin Collection Editions

*Please note: The number in brackets indicates the original Harlequin Romance number.*

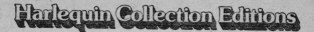
# Harlequin Collection Editions

*Please note: The number in brackets indicates the
original Harlequin Romance number.*

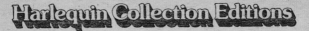
# Harlequin Collection Editions

*Please note: The number in brackets indicates the original Harlequin Romance number.*

# Complete and mail this coupon today!